MUTINY'S DAUGHTER

ANN RINALDI

Mutiny's Daughter

HarperCollins*Publishers*

Library of Congress Cataloging-in-Publication Data
Rinaldi, Ann.
Mutiny's daughter / Ann Rinaldi. — 1st ed.
    p. cm.
Summary: The story of half-Tahitian teenager Mary Christian, sent to the British
Isles to be raised by the family of her father, the British ship *Bounty*'s second in com-
mand and mutineer, Fletcher Christian.
    ISBN 0-06-029638-0 — ISBN 0-06-029639-9 (lib. bdg.)
    1. Christian, Fletcher, 1764–1793—Juvenile fiction. 2. Christian, Mary, 1793– —
Juvenile fiction. [1. Christian, Fletcher, 1764–1793—Fiction. 2. Christian, Mary,
1793– — Fiction. 3. Bounty Mutiny, 1789—Fiction. 4. Great Britain—History—
1789–1820—Fiction. 5. Fathers and daughters—Fiction. 6. Uncles—Fiction.
7. Racially mixed people—Fiction.] I. Title.
PZ7.R459Mu 2004
[Fic]—dc21

                                                                2003004447
                                                                        CIP
                                                                        AC

Typography by Nicole de las Heras
2 3 4 5 6 7 8 9 10

First Edition

To my sixth grandson, James Philip

Early in the morning as the sun rose in the eastern sky on the twenty-eighth of April, 1789, Fletcher Christian took over the HMS *Bounty* with some of his faithful friends. Christian had been second-in-command, and the ship had already been at sea for more than a year. By leading the mutiny, he made himself and his friends into mutineers, outlaws, and enemies of British King George III.

Fletcher Christian was twenty-four years old. And the man he mutinied against, Captain William Bligh, was loud, threatening, demanding, and cruel. It has become known as the most famous mutiny in history.

Christian knew what the results would be if he was

caught by English authorities. He would be dragged back to England in chains and hanged from a yardarm on a ship in the port of Spithead. But he wrote, and said to friends, "I am in hell."

The ship had just left Tahiti, where it had lingered for months while breadfruit specimens were collected to be brought to the West Indies. Christian and his followers put Captain Bligh and his sympathizers into a twenty-three-foot launch, with plenty of supplies but no compass, and set them adrift in the Pacific Ocean.

Then he guided the *Bounty* back to Tahiti, where some of the men wanted to stay. But Christian knew they would be discovered there, so he left Tahiti again, with his followers and some men and women from Tahiti, and went to seek another island. They found Pitcairn, an uninhabited island, and landed there in January 1790.

There they stayed for several years, establishing families and a community. Fletcher Christian had three children with a Tahitian woman named Mauatua, whom he renamed Isabella.

The children were Thursday October, Charles, and Mary.

The day Mary was born, in 1793, there was a massacre on the island, with the Tahitians killing the whites. It is said that on this day Fletcher Christian was killed, but no grave for him has been found on Pitcairn Island. Some say he was wounded and went to the other side of the island to recover from his injuries, then took the *Bounty*'s money and a cutter and rowed out to sea, where he met a ship bound for England. And popular legend, to this day, embraces the idea that he returned to England.

This novel asks the question "What if?"

What if Fletcher Christian brought his five-year-old daughter Mary with him when he finally returned? What if he brought her back to the Isle of Man, from whence he came, where his mother still lived, where his forebears had resided for over six hundred years? It is said that his children were "very handsome, their features strongly partaking of the English, the beauty of one of them, a girl named Mary, said to invite the same admiration which is favored of our own country-women."

"What if?" This is the question the novelist always asks—and, having asked it, starts to write.

⟋ O N E

1808

I dream, all the time, of ships. All kinds, from terribly large East Indiamen to sloops and packets and cutters. In these dreams, I am trying to board these ships, or rushing to meet them, or on one and passing others and searching. Searching for people whose names I do not know, running on the ships' decks, or packing, hastily, so I won't miss one. Packing is the worst. I can never fit everything into my trunk, and I am late.

Often, I am standing alone on the quay, having missed a cutter to take me out to a ship, standing with the most terrible feelings of dismay and anguish.

For the most part, in my dreams I have feelings of

anguish and distress and anxiousness, and failure. And loss. And if I take a voyage, I never arrive anywhere that I know. The place is always foreign to me. And nobody knows me. Nobody at all.

Of course, I have figured by now the cause of these dreams. They were born the day my father took me out to sea in the *Bounty*'s cutter. Away from that place where he'd lived for eight years in what was either a heaven or a hell of his own making. How long we floated in the sea in that cutter before we sighted the large ship that was to bring us to England, I do not know. For I have only my dreams. No memories.

I do not know how it happened, how my father sneaked me off that island, how he kept me from falling out of the cutter, I a child of only five, who was accustomed to roaming about the island with my older brothers at will, barefoot, free of spirit. Did I have shoes on my feet? Sandals? Did I wear a proper dress? If I did, did my mother make it? Out of what? Canvas sail? Or tapa, bark cloth, which my mother labored over for weeks to make fit for clothing?

I have been told that my father stole me away from my mother because he feared more killing of the children of white men on the island. He did not fear for my brothers, for they were already under the protection of the native man my mother was living with in the years my father was in hiding on the island. But he feared for me, for as a girl I was less valued, and I looked more English than Polynesian.

Did my father secure me to the seat of the cutter with ropes? How did he lift me to the great ship that took us on? How did he explain my manner of dress? Grandmother said the ship was American and that my father told the captain we'd been shipwrecked. But still, my dress. How did he explain that? Oh, how I wish I knew something solid so that when I go to sleep at night my dreams will have an end to them, or, if not, that I will have memory to build walls to contain them, their sights and sounds, their smells and feelings—to rein them in and end my anxiousness and fear.

Especially I wish I had the feeling of my father's arms around me, or the memory of his face next to mine, or even the words he must have said when Thursday October, my older brother, brought me to him from my mother's house on the other side of the island.

Where he must have said, "Come, little one, don't be afraid. Say good-bye to your brother now, and let us be gone from this place."

But I have none of it.

This seems so unfair.

I have asked Grandmother about it, but she won't answer. She won't speak of my father except when the mood seizes her. And when that happens, she is bitter and spends her words like shillings she doesn't want to part with.

"On the day you were born, in 1793, there was a massacre on the island," she will say. "Tahitian men killed the Europeans."

Then she finishes the story. "And your father was shot. How he survived, I do not know. I did not inquire."

My father brought me here in 1798. I am only fourteen.

He sneaked back to England, where he was thought of not only as a mutineer but also as a pirate, and a traitor to his King and his country.

He committed the worst sin our family could imagine. The sin of dishonor.

So the tale my grandmother and the others give out to the world is that my father, Fletcher Christian, was killed in the massacre on Pitcairn Island in 1793. And that his brother, Uncle Charles, is my father. That he begot me on a visit to the West Indies when he was in the merchant service.

I live that lie every day. And my grandmother lives in fear that I will give it away. And so do I.

⌒ T W O

The King sent men to the island of Tahiti to pursue my father. The King is George III, already half crazy. Captain William Bligh—the man my father mutinied against, the man my father put in a small boat with some of his men and set adrift in the Pacific Ocean— made it back to England, and was pardoned for any failure he had in the affair. For a while he was a hero in all of England and the isles, for traveling back over thousands of miles of sea in that small boat.

I happen to know that he didn't come right back to England. I have studied the whole sordid business, with the help of my uncle Charles, and without Grandmother's knowledge. Captain Bligh landed first on Timor, at Coupang, a Dutch settlement, where he refreshed himself. Then he sailed back to England.

My father was never found on Tahiti—because he wasn't there. He was on Pitcairn Island. Other mutineers were on Tahiti, and were arrested and brought back and court-martialed. Three were hanged. My uncle Edward wrote a book defending my father, but I hate Uncle Edward nevertheless, because he still acts as if my father has brought disgrace to this family. "There have been noblemen, statesmen, and rulers in this family for as far back as 1154 here on the Isle of Man!" he rages. "And now a mutineer!"

But sentiment is growing more and more in my father's favor every day. That's what Uncle Charles says. And I hear people whispering about my father. Saying that what he did was not an act of cowardice, but bravery. Stableboys whisper. People on the pier whisper. Milkmaids, shopkeepers. People who someday want their lot to be better. People who secretly applauded the revolutions in America and France. People who need to hope.

But no one in this family will hear of it. And Grandmother would have apoplexy if anyone found out that her granddaughter is Fletcher Christian's child by a Tahitian woman.

Why, I would not be able to go to the school in London she is sending me to in September if people knew! I would bring an agony of mind to Uncle Charles if anyone found out. And Uncle Charles is an esteemed physician hereabouts, and is good to me.

But oh, I would like to bring an agony of mind to Uncle Edward, if I had the chance! He has disapproved of me from the beginning.

He says I am "the perfect example of original sin." I would venture to say that he is. After all, it was he and my father's oldest brother, Uncle John (now dead), who spent all the family's money, so that Grandmother went bankrupt and my father had to go to sea in the first place.

Uncle Edward does not approve of my going to school in London, although he isn't paying for it. The Curwens are, with money my father entrusted to them for me. Isabella Curwen is one of my father's cousins. And it is their place we are going to visit this day, Belle Isle, their summer retreat on the mainland. My friend Langston Taubman is accompanying Grandmother and me.

Uncle Edward scoffed when he was last here and heard about the invitation.

"You're giving her ideas," he told Grandmother when he thought I was out of earshot. "It is never good to give the lower classes ideas."

"She's a Christian. Anything but lower-class. And you know Isabella Curwen has always taken an interest in her, and has had us to tea several times."

"You should discourage that interest. It bodes no good for anyone. You're not going to stay in their house, are you?"

"Mary is. I'm not. I'm staying with my sister on the mainland."

"The Curwens have supported you for years, Mother. I should think you wouldn't let them now start supporting Mary. Next they'll be giving her free milk, as they do the poor children in town."

The nerve of him! When he squandered all of Grandmother's money!

"They don't have a daughter of their own, Edward. Anyway, Isabella is going to instruct her on proper behavior in a fashionable London girls' school."

"Well, let's hope some good comes of it."

"Dearest, I know what you did for her father, with your position and your writings. And I am eternally indebted to you."

"I did it for us!" Uncle Edward whispered savagely. "For the family name!"

"She'll uphold it in school. She'll do us proud. I promise," Grandmother said.

"She had best, or she will answer to me, as head of the family!"

That is Uncle Edward. Chief Justice of the Isle of Ely, Professor of the Laws of England at Cambridge, Commissioner of Bankrupts (which he has much experience at), a Fellow of St. John's, Cambridge, and a dependable snob and stuffy dull wit.

He displays the family's coat of arms on his stationery and his carriage. SALUS PER CHRISTUM, it says. (That means "Health through Christ.") He is a leading barrister in London and lives there at Gray's Inn. I think the real reason he holds me in such low esteem is because now the Curwens have hold of my father's money, all the ducats from the *Bounty*. My father escaped with it. And Uncle Edward cannot get his hands on it as he got his hands on Grandmother's money.

But I cannot think of that now. I must get dressed. Langston will be here soon to accompany us across the water by packet boat.

⌒ THREE

"Mary, you can't leave until you have breakfast."

Grandmother came into my room, where I was sitting at my small desk, writing. I quickly closed my journal and stoppered the ink bottle. "I'm not hungry."

"A proper English girl always has breakfast."

Grandmother has been trying to make a proper English girl out of me for years, which means she scolds when I run about the quay to watch the herring boats come in and talk to the fishermen about their runs. I am very taken with the water.

"Have you packed?"

"Yes."

15

"Gwen is back. I'll send her up with a pot of tea, some black pudding, and scones. And Emily is packing a lunch for us on the packet."

"Gwen is back?" I turned, nearly knocking over the closed ink bottle. "When did she return?"

"Last evening! And I had all I could do to keep from taking a switch to her! I knew I should never have taken on that girl. Only out of deference to your uncle Charles have I done so!"

Uncle Charles was always attending to the poor and sick in and about our town of Douglas. Gwen Blundell was from a desperately poor family. Her father had been injured working on the Old Pier and was not able to work, and she had two little brothers. Uncle Charles had brought her home to help Grandmother five years ago. She was my own age, and we'd become friends. And oh, the things she knew!

"Where did she say she'd been for four days?" I asked Grandmother.

"Kidnapped by fairies."

Gwen believed in fairies. Like so many others on the isle, she clung to the folklore of fairies, elves, goblins, water horses, mermaids, and such. She believed that if you did a good troll a service, it would do you a helpful turn and you'd be lucky the rest of your life. She was forever looking for a good troll.

"Here, wear this blue dress. It goes so well with your golden skin. And it's made from the fabric Isabella brought back from London for you last season."

Grandmother was of two minds about Cousin Isabella Curwen. "If she hadn't wed John Curwen, your father never would have gone to sea," she always told me. "He signed on three months after she wed."

On the other hand, she knew she had to be grateful because Isabella's husband had helped her when she was going to be taken to Carlisle for Uncle Edward's and Uncle John's debts when my father was just a boy. And Isabella was always bringing things back from London for us. It made Grandmother uncomfortable.

She seldom said the woman's name. But there was another reason for that.

When my father married my mother on Pitcairn Island, he renamed her Isabella.

Grandmother set the dress down on my bed. "Don't keep Gwen long. A new lodger came last night, and I need her to attend to him."

Grandmother kept lodgers to make ends meet. Discreetly. People of importance who visited from the mainland were sent to her by John and Isabella Curwen. They had sent Langston, who was a poor distant relative of John's. Langston lived in a small upstairs room, worked with the herring fishermen in summers, and was like a brother to me.

When he wasn't working on the fishing boats this past summer, we spent the spare hours exploring the woods and fields, sneaking into ancient burial sites, fishing, setting snares for woodcock, even plundering birds' nests. We'd gathered hazelnuts, read the story of Robin Hood and *The Arabian Nights*.

"Now, don't you go chatting away with Gwen about her kidnapping," Grandmother said as she left the room. "You know how that girl lies. Likely she was off with Molly Carrooin's boy, Jed, and will turn up in the family way in a few weeks."

Not Gwen, I thought. She knows better. But I started to unbutton my nightgown to get dressed, and said nothing.

"The blue, oh yes, the blue." Gwen burst into the room and set down the tray. The whiff of tea nearly drove me daft, and I sat down immediately to have some. "Gwen, I'm so glad you're back." I got up to hug her. She smelled of wild berries, and her face was full of freckles from being out in the sun. "Were you truly kidnapped again?"

"Yes. Oh, it was dreadful!"

Of course, I didn't believe her, but I loved to hear about it. Besides, her eyebrows meet. And everybody on Man knows that if a person's eyebrows meet, that person has second sight. If such people go to church-yards on the eve of the New Year, or St. Mark's Day, or Midsummer's Day, they can tell you who will be buried there in the next year.

She went to the clothespress now and got out my best chemise.

"Tell me what happened, Gwen."

"I was goin' to market to get a pennyworth of tobacco for my father, passin' by a thornbush not far from your house, when I heard a loud crack, then a footstep. I thought it might be a good troll, but it was one of the fairies."

"Good or bad?"

"Not good. He shot an arrow at me. I collapsed. Then a whole bunch of them arrived, and when I came to, my feet would not suffer me to pass any farther. The fairies laid hold of me. One would let me go, but a quarrel ensued and they all became so angry they slapped me."

"Oh, no!"

She nodded solemnly. "Heartily. Only after they were through, they had no more power over me, so I ran home. I thought I was gone only a mornin', but it turned out to be four days. I showed my mother my back. I wanted to show it to your grandmother, too, but she refused to look or listen. Only scolded."

"Let me see." I stood up.

She undid her bodice and pulled up her chemise, and sure enough, there were small, bloody handprints all over her back that made it look as if she'd been slapped by fairies. "Gwen! Oh, Gwen!"

"And I can take you to that thornbush where they attacked me, too, and show you the blood on the stones."

"No," I said. But I offered her some tea and biscuits, which she took eagerly. "I'm going to ask if you can come with us today to Belle Isle," I offered.

"Are there trolls there?"

"I'm sure there are. It's the most beautiful place. And you'll love Lake Windermere."

"Your grandmother will never give permission. I'm behind in my work."

"I'll tell Grandmother that we must keep up appearances with the Curwens. That you must accompany me as my maid and chaperone."

She giggled. "You've been runnin' all over Man this summer, alone with Langston."

"I know. Can you imagine doing anything unseemly with Langston? Still, we must look proper. Lady Isabella expects propriety," I said. "I'll ask Grandmother. So go, put on your newest frock. I'll ask her right now."

"Of course she cannot go. I'm surprised at your even asking." Grandmother was in the dining room, at the table, having breakfast with a new gentleman lodger I didn't know and with Langston, who'd just come in from some errand. Langston stood up and bowed when I came into the room.

"Mary, you look so grown-up in that dress," he said. There was a teasing twinkle in his eye.

Langston was dressed in his best breeches and frock coat, and his shirt was ruffled at the neck. Grandmother herself had sewn the shirt for him. She coddled him more than she did me. More? She never coddled me, but then, all her "boys" were gone, except for Uncle Charles. And I saw sometimes how she looked at Langston when he was not paying mind. Is that the way she once used to look at my father?

"Alderman Hyden, this is my granddaughter, Mary." The man stood, bowed, and mumbled something. Introductions were quick. I curtsied. Grandmother got up, excused herself, and ushered me out of the room. "I told you not to encourage Gwen in such nonsense," she scolded in a hurried whisper. "Go get your cloak now, and wait for me in the lounge."

I went. Gwen deposited my baggage there, in the vestibule at the front of the house.

"I'm so sorry," I told her, though I knew one never apologized to servants.

"It's all right. I knew she wouldn't let me go. He's still supportin' her, you know. And she doesn't want to make it look like she's squanderin' his money, payin' a maid for you."

"Who?"

"Isabella's husband, John. Mr. Curwen. Him who changed his name from Christian to Curwen after Mrs. Christian's son did the mutiny."

I blushed. "You shouldn't say such, Gwen!" I told her sharply.

She bobbed a knee in a mock curtsy. "Everybody in town says such. I'm just repeatin' gossip. You know what else they're sayin'?"

"I'm fearful to ask."

"That her son who did the mutiny has been back in England."

"They've been saying that for a dozen years or so now." I somehow managed to keep my voice normal.

"Well," she sighed. "I look for him when I go out and explore the fells and the rocky places. With my luck, I'll find him before I find my good troll."

With your luck you will, I thought, and shivered. For I myself, every time I wandered on the quay or spoke to a fisherman, every time I roamed the woods and fields with Langston—I looked for him. Every time a privateer brought in a prize, I'd spy the captain and wonder if his face was dark enough for him to have lived on an island in the South Seas. Does he have that strange gait all the Christian men have, as Uncle Charles and Uncle Edward do? I'd ask myself. What is that shadow under that tree? Is that a red deer, or a man watching us? I'd stop running across a field to turn and see an empty space where the shadow had just been. And I'd shiver, afraid. For I was afraid of ever again meeting him. My own father.

"I'm going to take you on a trip with me someday, Gwen," I said. "I promise." I meant it. She deserved to go somewhere, and I just knew that someday I'd take her.

She smiled. I did not command respect from the servants, and it was my own fault. Truth to tell, I didn't command respect from anybody.

"Have a good time," she said. "As for me, I'm goin' to hunt for trolls when my work is finished. If it ever is." She rolled her eyes and ran from the room, and I gazed out the small leaded windows. The sycamore and beech trees cast shadows from the morning sun. I stepped outside and walked a distance from the house, and looked up at it. It comforted me, to see the only real house I'd ever lived in. It had two stories, was whitewashed, and had chocolate-colored crossbeams and brown shutters for ornamentation. The vestibule that jutted out in front was made of stone. In the back was a cottage where Uncle Charles had his surgery. He lived there, too—quite comfortably, surrounded by his books—ever since Grandmother had taken in lodgers. I saw him then, hitching up the carriage. Though we weren't far from town, he would take us to the dock to catch the packet. I waved, and he waved back.

A fence ringed the property, and in back were green hills, dotted with the Herdwick sheep Uncle Charles kept to help bring in money. The backdrop looked like one of the old tapestries that Grandmother had managed to bring here from Moorland Close, her manor house.

Uncle Charles brought the chaise around the drive, pulled up the horses, and stepped down. "Good morning, Mary."

"Good morning, sir."

It always had been easier for me to call him "sir" than "Father." I think he understood. He put his arm around me and kissed my cheek. "You have a good time on this trip now, hey? And enjoy Isabella. There's much you can learn from her. And you must do well in this school in London, Mary, or you'll end up back here making threepence a day spinning."

"I will, sir."

Uncle Charles was tall and thin yet muscular, with dark hair and deep brown eyes. Sometimes I fancied that he looked like one of the Vikings who had plundered the Irish Sea off the coast of Man in the tenth century. Or maybe like William Fletcher, one of Grandmother's ancestors, who had taken in Mary, Queen of Scots, when she fled her kingdom, and provided her with yards of red velvet to make into a dress so she could be properly attired when she was beheaded.

Uncle Charles had never wed. He was in his forties now, but I know the women all liked him, especially the ones who came to his surgery with pretended ailments. They were a plague to him, he said.

He took his role as my surrogate father seriously. He appeared at my school in town for recitations, took me to fairs and harvest celebrations, stood beside me and Grandmother in St. George's Church on Sundays, and sometimes let me accompany him on his rounds when he visited patients.

But he was a stern taskmaster, insisting I do well in school and respect my grandmother. Many a time I was sent by Grandmother to his lodgings after some mischief or wrongdoing.

There was honesty between us. On these occasions, though he always managed to deliver a proper scolding or mete out a sufficient punishment, always he would finish with "Mary, I'm not your father. I wish I were. And I dearly wish he were here. But I'm going to do my best for his daughter in his stead."

He had been to sea. To Madras, on an East Indiaman, a merchant vessel. He had been a ship's surgeon, yet he knew the use of a ship's charts and instruments. In his cottage he had a chest made of teak. He'd shown me the contents once. Madras cloth. Soft white fabric, yards of it, like handkerchiefs for giants. A rope of coconut hair. Cunning tins of exotic bohea tea, which he'd give to Grandmother or me if we were feeling ill. It took four to six weeks each way to and from the East Indies, he'd told me.

He was the only one who would ever speak to me of my real father, of the things they'd done together as boys, of the way he'd met my father in the channel when my father was on the *Bounty* sailing out and Uncle Charles was on the *Middlesex* sailing into Spithead. How my father had taken a small boat out to the *Middlesex* and they'd spent all night long talking. "Your father was strict with the men under him at sea," he said, "but he made toil a pleasure and ruled over them in a pleasant manner."

He's showed me, too, how he and my father both crossed their *t*'s in the same manner.

He smiled, but said nothing, when I first told him that one of my brothers on Pitcairn had been given the name of Charles. Uncle Charles was a dear and good man, and I loved him.

"Ah, here comes your grandmother," he said now. He had always stood by Grandmother. He rushed forward to help Langston with her trunks. The only other men we had about the place were Frank—husband to

Bridget, our cook—who did the heavy work in the house and acted as butler for the men guests; Ralph, the sheepherder; and Emmett, who ran the farm. Many was the time I'd seen Uncle Charles bring a bucket of coal up from the cellar for the fireplaces.

He settled us in the carriage, with a rug around Grandmother's legs lest she take cold, and we started for the quay.

⌒ FOUR

We stayed the night in Whitehaven, at the Lion's Cub Inn, after disembarking the packet. At supper, in the dining room, Langston gave me a kick under the table and I knew what he wanted. He wanted to talk to me in private. I sensed there were things he wanted to tell me before we went to Belle Isle.

"Grandmother, aren't you tired? Shall I see you to bed?"

But she would not leave the table. She was sullen. Even though Langston lived in our house, she still did not trust us alone together. So she and I retired early to bed, and Langston stayed by the roaring fireplace with some other travelers and ordered himself a mug of grog like a grown man. And I was so jealous of him. Oh, I wished I were a boy!

In the morning, we boarded the post chaise for Cockermouth, the town where my father had spent his boyhood. Grandmother's mood persisted, and I supposed it was because memories were closing in on her. In the carriage, she bent herself to her reading. Without raising her eyes from her book, she pointed out landmarks.

"There is St. Bee's, where your father went as a young man," she said as we left Whitehaven.

Then she fell into silence again, and I hoped the rocking of the post chaise would make her fall asleep. But she kept right on reading. It was at least a dozen miles to Cockermouth, so I decided to enjoy the countryside. Soon, in the distance, I could see Skiddaw.

"Doesn't Wordsworth live around here with his sister Dorothy?" Langston asked.

"Wordsworth!" Grandmother said scornfully. "A useless example of English decadence."

"He's a great poet," Langston insisted.

"Grandmother doesn't like him," I put in.

"Why?"

But I did not answer. Grandmother did. "Great poet, indeed! He used to tarry at our gate, begging for some tarts. My son Edward was his schoolmaster for a year at Hawkshead Grammar School. Couldn't keep a thing in his head."

"He's friends with Coleridge, and may even have helped him write *The Rime of the Ancient Mariner.*" Langston was pushing his point too far, and from where I sat, across from him, I kicked his shin. But he ignored me and said to Grandmother, "Aren't you proud that such a grand poem was written about your son Fletcher?"

A chill went through me. How dare he! But he knew what he might and might not dare with Grandmother. Still not looking up from her book, she said, "Prithee. 'Twasn't about Fletcher."

"People say it is," Langston insisted. He had charm, he did, with his curly chestnut hair and blue eyes. Grandmother took from him what she'd never take from me. But now, still without looking up from her book, she rapped his ear. "Insolent boy! I say it isn't. People say a lot of things."

The ride to Cockermouth went quickly. When we arrived, Grandmother finally put her book down.

"There is Cockermouth Free Grammar School. And there is a funeral. Take off your hat."

Langston did so. The driver stopped the horses on the cobblestone street to let the funeral cortege pass in front of some whitewashed cottages on Kirkgate, by the Derwent River. The heads of the horses pulling the funeral carriage were decorated with black plumes, the carriage had large glass windows, and the women walking behind it were dressed in silk finery.

"It must be somebody important," Langston said.

"Can't be, or I'd have heard," Grandmother said. "It's likely a farmer." And after we had continued on a bit, she said, "There's the house your uncle John once owned."

It was massive. "It's very elegant," I said.

"It has seventeen bedrooms. He mortgaged it against Moorland Close, and I lost the place. But the Curwens saved us. Remember that when you visit."

After we passed the small houses close to the river, which she said were owned by tanners and weavers, the countryside widened. I saw farms and distant fields filled with haycocks; tall grain waiting for the harvest; dark, inviting woods; neat hedges around redbrick houses; late-summer roses; ivy clinging to archways;

beech and oak trees guarding gates. To the east were the old towers of Cockermouth Castle, which was now in ruins.

Then, as we were about to pass a two-story house of blue stone and tile, she ordered the driver to stop. "Here is where I stay," she told us.

"Grandmother, you're not even coming to Belle Isle for tea?" I asked.

"Cross Lake Windermere? Not if I don't have to! See John and Isabella? Not if I don't have to! Help me to the door, young man," she ordered Langston.

Langston jumped down, helped her out of the post chaise, and carried her trunk to the door. Just as they got to it, a man came rushing down the path, waving what looked like a letter. I saw him confer with Grandmother for a minute or so and saw her give him a coin. Then the man left. Langston stayed with her while she opened the letter. Then she gave him some last-minute orders and a small leather bag that he put in his pocket.

"She's a grand old lady, your grandmother," he said, getting back into the post chaise. "She's a hellion."

"What did she give you?"

"Orders that if I didn't behave with you, she'd

skin me alive. And gold sovereigns for the boat and a tip for our chaise driver." Then Langston told the driver to make haste and get us to the water's edge at Windermere.

"What was in the letter?"

"It came from Man, from your uncle Charles. Gwen is missing again."

"Why would Uncle Charles write to Grandmother? Gwen has been missing before."

"Because she ran off the minute we left. And they think she's lost."

I drew in my breath. "She's looking for trolls. She knows what she's about." But I wished I believed it.

"What have you been wanting to tell me?" I asked Langston as he rowed us across Lake Windermere. The water was calm, and in the distance were the empty sails of a few boats. In the west, the late-August sun was losing itself behind the mountains, and small islands of dark woodland to the east were already full of night.

"Well, for one thing, I think Uncle John is going to ask me to keep an eye out for you in London when you go to school. I will be attending Cambridge and would come down to visit from time to time. Would you mind?"

"Are you going to tattle if I do something bad?"

"Are you planning on it?"

His face was so serious that for the moment I could see the man he would one day be. And it looked a lot like John Curwen. "Of course," I said.

Then he broke into a smile. I giggled, and soon we were laughing together.

"There's something else I wanted to tell you," he said. I was still laughing when he said it. "I think Uncle John is my father."

I stopped laughing then, and just stared at him. "Your mother was a sister of his first wife," I said. Isabella's husband John had been married before. His first wife had died.

He nodded. "You remember the last political meeting he had at Workington Hall, when he told everyone assembled how he felt like a father to them all?"

"I've heard tell of it."

"Well, did you hear tell how one woman cried out that he was indeed father to half the town of Cockermouth?"

I blushed. "I heard. Grandmother heard, too, and was very mortified."

"Well," he said again, "I do think he's my father."

"Did he tell you?"

"No, but I've heard things."

I fell silent. Our boat went through some tall reeds in the water. In the distance, on the small dock at Belle Isle, I saw a figure holding a lantern.

"It must be terrible not being able to acknowledge your own father," I said to Langston.

He was rowing slowly now, and as he leaned forward with the oars, his eyes met mine. "Yes," he said. "I knew you would understand, Mary." Though Langston had never told me that he knew Fletcher Christian was my father, I think he did know. How could he not? He was a ward of John Curwen's, and often privy to the man's private affairs. Oh, it was difficult, wondering who knew and who didn't! It was a web of secrets, and always I felt as if I were walking on eggs when I was with people.

Then I looked up and saw a man on a small ramp, holding the lantern. Loons called, and a few white swans glided by the edge of the lake. It was so peaceful. And in the distance, behind the waiting man, was the domed roof of the house on Belle Isle, all lighted with candles as dusk closed in. Langston expertly maneuvered the small boat between reeds and water lilies to the dock, and threw the line of rope to the waiting man.

At close inspection, the man proved to be a servant I had not seen before at the Curwens'. He wore a white wig tied in the back, black breeches, and a frock coat. Was he elderly? If so, why were his eyes so young? I noticed, too, that he limped.

"Mr. Taubman and Miss Christian?" he asked. And he helped us out of the boat and onto the landing. "The Curwens await your arrival."

They tell me that when my father brought me to Grandmother's house on the Isle of Man and then left, I cried for a month. I have some memory of it. I recollect sitting in a big chair in Grandmother's parlor and sobbing, but I do not remember the feeling of it. I do not recollect why I was crying.

They tell me it was because I missed my mother. Today I do not remember my mother.

But when I was sitting in that big chair in Grandmother's parlor, sobbing, a beautiful lady came in. And she talked to me. She had some lovely clothes for me, and a doll. I do remember that.

That lady was Cousin Isabella Curwen.

After that, I stopped crying.

All my life I'd admired Isabella Curwen. Her soft ways, her manner of enclosing you in her love. Her caring nature. And then, later, I came to admire her riches, her beauty, the entertainments she hosted in London when she went there with her husband, who was a member of Parliament.

How I wished she were my mother!

Every time Grandmother brought me for a visit, I became newly enamored of Isabella. She had been in love with my father when she was young, perhaps as young as I am now. She'd been forbidden to marry him. That was all I knew. But that was enough for me now. It had to be.

I'd followed her doings, her attendance at the Royal Opera, her shopping expeditions for the latest Windsor fashions, her attendance at court and balls and masquerades.

On the Isle of Man, and here in the Lake Country, she was a fairy princess, more famous than Queen Charlotte.

And there was a warm place inside me, just knowing she was in the background of my life.

As we followed the limping servant through the marble-floored hallways of Belle Isle, out to the back terrace where the Curwens waited, my eyes wandered. No matter how many times I'd been here, I saw something new each time. All around, there were wide windows that brought the pleasures of the outside in. And from windows on the western side of the house, the full beauty of the red-and-purple sunset flooded the fields and gardens. A winding stairway went to the upper floor. Chinese porcelain was in great supply. Oriental rugs were underfoot; a piano held a large candelabra. A portrait of Isabella hung over the marble mantel of a fireplace, and there were tapestries of knights of old, oil paintings of people who were likely related to Grandmother—lords, earls, justices, who had ruled and protected, who owned ancestral homes, sailed with flotillas, and headed clans for hundreds of years.

There was money here, from mining and shipping interests. I knew that much.

"Here they are. Welcome, children." It was John who came to greet us. He kissed me and shook hands with Langston. I kissed Cousin Isabella, and remembered to curtsy. "Thank you for having us, ma'am."

"Dear child," Isabella said warmly. "Where is your grandmother? Didn't she come?"

"She was tired and went to stay at the house of her sister."

"Oh, of course, poor thing. Come, come, sit, children. You must be starved. Adian, bring some scones and sugared apples and jellies, and some small meat pies. I know how young people can eat. Please sit. We've decided to have our repast here instead of in the dining room." And with a taper, Adian went about lighting rushes in tall iron lanterns that ringed the terrace. He was the same limping servant who had met us at the dock.

We sat around a wrought-iron table, in chairs with flowered cushions. Two large dogs lay nearby. A cat lying near my ankles purred. Grandmother never allowed pets in the house.

"How was the crossing in the Whitehaven packet and the row across the lake?" John asked Langston.

They talked. As Adian brought our repast and set it out, John did a peculiar thing. He introduced us to him. "Adian, our butler, is a trusted servant," he said. "Ask him for anything while you are here."

Adian poured my tea. As he did so, he leaned over me. His eyes met mine and held them for a minute, and I felt a moment's calm. "I'd love to see the flower gardens," I said. They lay on either side of the path that wound to the lake. Butterflies hovered over them, and statues of elves and nymphs were placed about. "This place is like heaven," I said.

Isabella put her hand over mine. "We're going to have a lovely time," she said.

⌐— F I V E

We were to stay for three days, visiting, walking around the island, romping with the dogs, fishing, reading—even riding the horses the Curwens kept for their own pleasure. I made friends with the parrot, Samuel Johnson.

That parrot! Isabella was very literary, and so had named him after England's man of letters. Samuel kept us laughing by quoting snatches of Shakespeare. And, as I passed by his elegant cage, he'd say: "Don't let her find out. Don't let her find out."

I'd stop and look at him, and ask, "Don't let who find out what?"

And he'd blink at me innocently and quote Shakespeare.

Then, when I walked away, he'd say, "No profit in it, no profit in it. Don't let her find out. No profit in it."

Was he teasing? Or repeating something he'd heard? I asked Adian, who laughed. "Oh, the mistress has many important ladies to dine. No doubt he's repeating gossip," he said.

I made friends with Adian. I have a habit, disdained by Grandmother, of making friends with the servants. Adian took me into the gardens that grew on the slope that led down to the lake. I marveled at the flowers, still blooming in late summer. The garden was a feast for the eyes. "There are even late roses," I said. "I love roses!"

"I'll cut you some when you leave," he promised.

Evenings Isabella played the piano, and we read *Maria* by Mary Wollstonecraft. Isabella was very forward-thinking in her views about the education of women. And in the background, as we read, I could hear John discussing the plight of the "climbing boys" in London. I didn't know what climbing boys were. Isabella told me.

"Chimney sweeps. Their lot is a terrible one,

although bills have been put through in the House of Lords to improve it. My husband is working with magistrates to help them."

I wished I could stay forever in this magical place. Isabella even had an aviary where she kept pet birds. Oh, how I wished the Curwens would let me live with them! Grandmother's house was so dark and forbidding. The only good things there were Uncle Charles, Gwen, and the farm animals. As I prepared for bed on the second night, I was determined to entertain the fancy in my head when there came a rap on the door and Isabella entered, wearing a blue gown with a polonaise.

"Darling, we're having late guests. I'll likely be sleeping in the morning. But you'll be leaving, I'm afraid. A note came around from your grandmother."

Gwen had still not been found, and Grandmother had decided to cut short her visit and go home. We must leave early in the morning.

"Oh, I feel so guilty! I've completely forgotten Gwen!" I cried. I sat down on the bed, tears streaming down my face. "I've had such a good time here and lived so luxuriously, and poor Gwen is out looking for trolls to improve her luck!"

"She'll be found," Isabella promised. "But Mary,

since I won't see you in the morning, there are things I must tell you."

I pricked up my ears and dried my eyes. "Is it about my father? Have you seen him?"

She blushed. "No, dear. It's about school in London."

"Would you tell me if you saw him, if he came around to visit you?"

"Now, why would he come here?"

Because you once loved him, I wanted to say, but I dared not say it.

She looked away for a moment, then continued, "Women give birth to the world, Mary. Over and over again. Every day. And men don't even know it. But women—by their striving and daily activities, from cooking and mending to freshening and peacemaking, feeding, planning, sacrificing, and hoping; and by not dying from hurt and disappointment but going on—give birth to the world every day."

I stared at her. "Is that what you wanted to tell me?"

"In part." She stroked my hair. "I don't expect you to understand that now. What I really meant to say is that when you go to this school in London, you must behave with propriety at all times. You see, dear, it's a progressive school for girls. And it is watched very closely. Not one whiff of scandal must touch it. Not one whiff!"

Her blue eyes were steady and unblinking as they met mine. "Do you take my meaning?" she asked.

"Yes," I said. "I mustn't let anyone there know that Fletcher Christian is my father."

She put her arms around me then and hugged me tightly. "Dear child, you are so dear to me. And to my husband, John. He is a man of good parts, and he trusts that you will do right by us in London. And by your family. That you will keep the family honor."

That again. "I hate the family honor," I said.

She gasped. "Mary, don't say such."

"What is the purpose of it?"

"It is the price you pay for your station. It is what people expect from you. It is the debt you incur for being of the upper class."

"I'm not of that class."

"Yes, you are, through your father."

"Grandmother says he didn't keep the family honor."

"He did. I promise you, he did. Under the circumstances, he did his utmost to keep it."

I bowed my head. "All right, I will keep it, too," I said.

"Now, the two mistresses of the school, Sophia and Harriet Hartsdale, are old schoolgirl friends of mine, you know. They believe in the teachings of Mary Wollstonecraft. They are successful writers and know many other women writers who have advocated the rights of women — Joanna Southcott, Ann Radcliffe, and others."

"Do they know Coleridge?"

"I'm not sure."

"I'd like to meet him," I said.

"Perhaps it will be possible. But the thing is, you must remember that things are not easy for women today. Advances are being made, but quietly, and if any scandal is attached to anyone making them, we will be put instantly back into the Dark Ages."

"I understand," I said.

We said our good-byes.

When I awoke in the morning, one of Isabella's maids was standing by my bed, holding a tray with my breakfast. Outside, mists circled the house, like the ones that Mannanan-Beg-Mac-y-Leir covered the island of Man with in the fifth century in order to keep strangers away. When people approached the isle, what did they see in the mist? A hundred times the number of warriors there actually were, opposing their landing.

The mist wrapped around Langston and me as we got into the boat. And, true to his word, Adian stood by, a bouquet of roses in his hand. As I stepped into the boat, he handed them to me. "Your favorites from the gardens, Miss Christian," he said.

I was touched. For some reason, tears came to my eyes as I took them.

"Good luck in school. You'll do well."

He was looking at me so closely, with such sincere meaning, that I reached up from the boat and put my arms around his slender form. Slender, I thought, but not old, no. I felt the strength in him encircling me. He kissed my forehead, then backed away. "Forgive me," he said. "You remind me of someone."

"Thank you," I said again.

"It has been an honor serving you. Come back again."

Something about him there was, something that made me shiver. Something about the whole place, some fragile beauty it had that made me think it would someday vanish, always made me shiver. Adian stood watching, waving his hand in farewell as Langston rowed away, until I could see him no more for the mist that draped us and wrapped us in silence. The only sound was the dipping of the oars into the water. For about half an hour, Langston and I seemed lost in a world of our own.

"How can you know the way?" I asked him tremulously.

"I've been across this water so many times," he said.

On the opposite shore, I expected to see hundreds of warriors, opposing our landing. But as we approached, all I saw was the outline of Grandmother's post chaise, the horses stamping in impatience, the driver standing by them, waiting. And Grandmother inside, grumpier than ever.

"There have been parties out searching for Gwen," Grandmother said. "Your uncle Charles writes that every man, woman, and child in Douglas has been traipsing through fells, woods, graveyards, ruins, and caves, but she has not been found. Oh, and I promised her parents she would be safe if she came and worked for us! That poor girl, out in the open for three nights! And they've not been warm ones. Driver, proceed!" She rapped on the window. "We must catch the eleven-o'clock packet!"

Grandmother's concern startled me.

The day, which had started out misty, soon cleared. Langston and I walked the deck of the packet while Grandmother huddled inside the cabin. "Oh!" I exclaimed as I clutched Langston's hand. "The sky is so blue! The sun so bright! It's exciting just to be alive, isn't it?"

"You're still seized with the magic of Belle Isle," he said.

"It is magic there, isn't it? Didn't you love the aviary? Isabella's parrot, Samuel Johnson, is almost human!"

"Everything about Isabella is magic," he agreed. "But unfortunately, now we must face the real world. Both of us off to school. I in two days, and you in a week. And this dolorous business with Gwen. Did she give you any hints as to where she might have gone off to, Mary?"

I felt ashamed of momentarily forgetting Gwen. "All she ever said was that she was looking for good trolls."

"That could take her anywhere."

We were coming into Douglas Bay, and as many times as I'd made this approach to home, it always took my breath away. To the northeast of us was the headland of Banks Howe, and to the southwest the bold outline of Douglas Head, jutting out into the sea. In the center of the bay was Conister Rock, onto which many vessels had run in bad weather. Uncle Charles always said that we needed a beacon there for the safety of ships, and he was working with Sir William Hillary Bart, who was so concerned about shipwrecks, to get one built.

In the background, the surrounding countryside rose to majestic heights: hills, woods, and general grandeur. My heart lifted with hope every time I saw it. I did not know what Pitcairn Island, where I was born and once lived, looked like. But Uncle Charles told me there was no more beautiful place on earth than the Isle of Man, and I believed him.

"I wish I had a spyglass," I said to Langston.

"What for?"

"I want to spy the nunnery."

"Why are you so fascinated with that place?"

We leaned on the packet's railing as I told him. "It is said that people who went there for cures always recovered. And that when the laws of the place were violated, the prioress put the offenders into hollows in the steep rocks, at the place called Pigeon Stream. The lower hollow caught the incoming tide, and the poor nun put there had to remain until the tide flowed and ebbed twice. If she lived, she was proven innocent, but if she didn't, she was accounted guilty."

"I suppose Gwen told you all these stories."

"Oh, yes, and more. She said those hollows in the rocks are wonderful places to hide."

I stopped my chatter then and looked at Langston, and he at me. Finally he spoke. "If someone was hiding there, she couldn't be found." His voice cracked. "Those rocks at Pigeon Stream rise two hundred feet above sea level."

My own voice was a whisper. "Could someone climb up there?"

"If she was looking for good trolls, she could."

Then he hurried off.

"Where are you going, Langston?"

"To ask the captain for the loan of a spyglass."

Langston peered through the glass. I stood next to him. Grandmother stood behind us as he scanned the horizon.

"I've sighted Pigeon Stream," he said quietly. "Dear God, the rocks above it are sharp and jagged."

"Pray," Grandmother said.

"There are dozens of people on the pier!" Langston noted. And then he let out with a "Ho! I've spotted something."

"What? What?" we begged.

"Looks like a seabird. Are there red seabirds?"

We both said no.

"Well, it's a bit of red. There, in a hollow in the rocks. It looks like— Yes, it's a signal from someone. Someone is waving it to get our attention. Holy Mother of God, it's a girl, I think!"

The spyglass went from one to another. I tried to steady it in front of my eye. I could scarcely make out the face of the person in the hollow far above Pigeon Stream, but I was sure it was Gwen.

"Oh, Langston, we've found her!"

Langston ran to the captain again, and soon we were making all possible speed to the harbor. On the way, the captain sounded a shot for Gwen to let her know she'd been seen and would soon be rescued. When we got to the pier and dropped anchor, the crowd raised a shout. They'd been standing for hours, it turned out, hoping some boat would sight Gwen from the bay.

Immediately, fishermen, constables, weavers,

farmers—all kinds of people, of high and low station—held a conference on the pier. And standing on a barrel, leading them, was Uncle Charles!

"We'll take the strongest boat," he was shouting to choruses of "mine, mine!" "I've been in those waters!" "The time is right! The sea is calm!"

Three boats were selected, lest one or more get dashed on the rocks. Strong coils of rope were thrown aboard, and a man came forward who said, in a Cockney accent, that he was an English sailor. "A real Jack-tar, I am. If anybody kin climb those rocks, it's me."

They elected him to do the climbing. Uncle Charles went with his medical bag. A woman came up with warm blankets and a jar of soup. In the distance I saw Gwen's father in his wheelchair, his two small boys clinging to him, his wife behind him.

"About halfway around the point," said the English sailor, "at low water, there is a landing place."

A huzzah went up from those left on the pier, and pipes were sounded, and the rescuers were off.

We waited. The rectors of St. George's Church and St. Matthew's Chapel came to the pier and led us in prayer. A man from a nearby inn brought us hot coffee, and meat and scones. Farmers said they hoped the rescue would be soon; they had their evening milking to get done. Someone said that when Gwen got back, the church bells should be rung. The rectors agreed.

One woman objected. "Wouldn't that be celebrating the mischief of a young girl of light character, then?" she asked.

"She is not of light character." It was Grandmother who stepped forward. Everyone in town knew Grandmother. She was a Christian, and Christians had run this isle for six hundred years. "She works for me. She is a protégée of my son, Dr. Charles Christian. Her parents are good and honest people. I say ring the church bells, if God is good enough to bring her back to us."

"She believes in witchcraft," this same woman said. "Just last week, she was going about saying she was kidnapped by fairies."

"Most of the children on this isle believe in its folk-lore," Grandmother answered. "And it's a grand and lovely tradition."

A murmer of assent rose from the crowd. "The church bells will be rung," said the Reverend Forbes, the rector of St. George's.

I squeezed Grandmother's hand, and brought her to a bench on the pier to sit, and with the others we waited.

The boats came back in a little over two hours, to cheers from the waiting crowd. Gwen was carried off one of them by none other than Uncle Charles. She was wrapped in blankets, and he put her in his gig and took her right off to home, with her parents following.

I'd been so proud of Grandmother and the way she'd stood up to certain people on the pier. But I should have known that she would. She was speaking up for the family honor because Uncle Charles was involved in the rescue. Now, back home, she settled into her usual mood. She would not speak of the matter to me. After I was upstairs in bed, that night, I heard her arguing softly with Uncle Charles. I crept out of bed, making sure all the lodgers were snoring, and leaned over the railing. They were discussing Gwen.

"You must let her come back," Uncle Charles said. "If only for our own protection. You know she knows all about us."

"Must we live under such fear, then?" Grandmother asked.

"I prefer to call it insurance," Uncle Charles said.

Grandmother pursued her argument. "And how she found out all about us is what I wish to know. Did you ever ask her?"

All I could see belowstairs was the light cast by candles. I longed to run down to Uncle Charles and thank him for whatever it was he had done for Gwen, but of course I did not. All I did was listen.

"I did ask. She says the fairies told her."

"And you believe such rot?"

"I don't know what I do or do not believe anymore, Your Ladyship." It was the way he addressed Grandmother when he was being very formal. "All I know is that the child needs the work and the family needs her earnings. And certainly we can afford to keep her."

Then he went out into the night, around the house to his cottage in back, and to whatever solace its loneliness and his books gave him.

Gwen was back in two days, in time to ready my clothing to be packed. Langston had left for school in London right after our trip to the mainland. Uncle Charles was to take me to London at the end of the week.

Isabella had sent me a parcel of clothing by packet on the day after we had left. Warm skirts, gloves, silk slippers—even two chemise-style dresses with scooped-out necks and high waistlines in the latest fashion.

Nightgowns of the softest wool, and a new cape. Gwen looked at me enviously as she packed my things in a trunk and I got together my favorite books, my pearl-handled comb and brush, my special doll that Isabella had given me the day she first met me, a shell I'd managed to collect from Pitcairn Island the day I left with my father, and a scrap of tapa cloth from a dress my father had brought along for me on our voyage.

Gwen had not yet spoken of her disappearance, but I knew she was waiting for me to ask.

"I'll miss you," she said.

"And I, you." I kneeled on the bed. "Tell me what happened. They say you nearly died."

"Oh, I did, but the good troll I met kept me alive."

"Tell me."

She stopped folding my things and walked back and forth in front of the window, her arms folded against her bosom. "Well, I climbed the rocks. There are places to climb, you know. I just knew I'd find a good troll. I felt him watching for me as I climbed. And by the time I got to the top, sunset was coming on, and it was so beautiful that I lingered. Then I decided to climb back down. But my foot missed a ledge and I slipped down, down, into a great hole."

"Oh, Gwen!"

"I could hear the sea splashing and the gulls crying, but it was so black! I finally got purchase on a ledge, but it was so narrow! I had to hold on to another piece of rock above me, and there I stood all night. How fearful I was of falling asleep! And how cold! But I prayed, oh, I prayed! And then I saw the good troll, peering over the top of the rock at me.

"'If you can hold on, you will survive,'" he told me. "'And I will give you luck throughout your life.' And then he laughed and disappeared. Well, he made me so angry I did hold on! I could glimpse the water through a crack in the ledge. I even saw a boat or two, with lanterns, but no one could hear my cry from up there. So I hung on all night."

"How?"

"I don't know. I think if you want to hang on, you can. I think sometimes that wanting is part of it. Or maybe all of it. Then morning came, and all I could think of was my tremendous thirst. I wanted water so bad, I'd have dashed myself into the sea for some! Except that I knew I couldn't drink that."

"'Water, water every where,'" I said, "'nor any drop to drink.'"

"Now, where did you get that?"

"From *The Rime of the Ancient Mariner* by Coleridge."

"Yes, well, did he ever hang from a rock all night?"

"I think not."

"Well, on a small ledge nearby were some shells. And a break in the rock from which water was dripping. I didn't know if I could get a shell and fill it with some water without dashing myself to bits on the rocks below, but I tried. And I managed to do so. And the water was fresh, and not salt. And I had some to restore myself. But still I waited and prayed, and by noon of the fourth day I spied a boat coming into the harbor."

"Our packet," I said.

"Yours?" She blinked at me. Then she said, "Yes, your Uncle Charles told me how you and Langston spied me through the glass. I took my scarf from my neck and waved it, still holding on desperately with one hand. It was my only chance. When I heard the shot, my heart leaped with hope! But then I still had hours to wait, not knowing for sure if anyone would come to fetch me."

"Did the troll come back?"

"Yes. Once. He told me I had done well. That he would favor me with luck, but I must know that life is hard. Not because it is meant to be, but because our fellow man makes it hard, one for the other. And he had a message for me."

"What?"

"He said that someday soon I would take a trip with my best friend, to a faraway place."

"London?" I asked.

"No. He said farther away than that."

"Oh, Gwen!" We hugged, but I did not believe what she had said. How could I be going farther than London? And why?

We parted at the end of the week, each sensing it was the end of an old way of life. But what would the new one be? And what of Gwen's message from the troll?

I wished I weren't starting to believe her.

SIX

The last thing Grandmother said to me when I left for school with Uncle Charles was "Don't get mixed up with the bluestockings in London."

Then she kissed me, and sighed. "London! To think I'm sending you there! It is a wart on the face of humanity."

The trip took two days. Uncle Charles wanted to give me a tour of the great city of London before he accompanied me to my new school. We stayed overnight at an inn on the mainland, then boarded a coach for our inland journey. Thank heaven the only other passenger was an elderly gentleman, who introduced himself as Mr. Fettlestone and struck up a conversation with Uncle Charles immediately about the Irish Rebellion in 1798. Then he promptly fell asleep, so I could talk to Uncle Charles. I knew it would be my last chance to do so for a while, so I took full advantage of it.

"What are bluestockings, Uncle Charles?" I asked.

"You know you're supposed to call me 'Papa' when we're out."

"He's asleep."

"Nevertheless. And I shan't answer a single question otherwise."

"Yes, sir. Papa. So then, what are bluestockings?"

He sighed, sensing a long session. I know he was hoping to read his copy of *The Times*, but he folded it up and tucked it beside him on the seat. As always, he was ready to instruct. And as always, he expressed himself very handsomely.

"They are women who dedicate themselves to the notion that women are equal to men in the matter of brains."

"Is that bad?"

"Don't be facetious, Mary."

"No, I mean it seriously, sir."

Another sigh. "They are intellectual, artistic, and very sociable. They promote female accomplishments.

But they can be dangerous. In London, many such people are watched, for fear that they are promoting rebellion. And since the French Revolution, they have been suspect. Which is why your grandmother cautioned you. And I caution you now. I think the schoolmistresses themselves have such leanings. Listen to them and learn from them, but do not do anything to promote their radical philosophy."

"Yes, sir. What's wrong with female accomplishment?"

"Nothing, Mary. We wouldn't allow you to go to this school if we thought there was. In London today there are women jailkeepers, newspaper owners, playwrights, and the like. But there is a way of accomplishing your ends without flaunting them. We hope knowing the difference will be part of your education."

"Cousin Isabella said the school has running water. Is that true?"

"Yes. It's pumped in from the Thames, though it runs only three times a week. Best not to drink it. Now, your school is in the West End, where many fashionable people live. No doubt you'll be mixing with them. Many help the school. But if you come home all superior, with your nose in the air, I shall switch you."

I smiled. He had never so much as raised a hand to me. "I promise I will keep my nose grounded, sir. I wouldn't know how to act superior."

"I know, Mary. Still, you must hold yourself to your family's honor. So you've got some hard work ahead of you. You've had enough of a good example from Grandmother, and you've certainly got the clothing now."

"I've got a chocolate-colored silk gown with a polonaise," I said. "Isabella had it made for me."

"I'm sure you'll look beautiful in it."

"May I ask something else?"

"Ask away."

"Why is Grandmother so unkind sometimes?"

A frown, then another sigh. "She was a widow at age thirty-six, Mary." He took his hat off the seat and turned it in his hands, as if to examine it. "She was left with six children, from age fourteen to three months. She lived the life of a lady as a child and young woman. She was an heiress. Her mother was a Fletcher. Moorland Close was hers. And now she lives in a farmhouse, and takes in lodgers. Her son Humphrey died when he heard the news of Fletcher's mutiny. You know that."

"Yes, sir."

"Would you not be a little bitter at her age?"

"I meant no disrespect, sir."

He nodded. He never countenanced my not reverencing Grandmother.

"Is it true that your father's grandfather was Queen Anne's solicitor?"

Next to him on the seat, the elderly gentleman snored loudly all of a sudden, snorted and coughed, and leaned toward Uncle Charles as the coach rounded a curve. Uncle Charles righted him before answering.

Then: "Yes, it's true."

"May I tell the other girls that?"

"I said not to act superior, Mary."

"But girls boast. And I can only imagine what sort they will be here. If I *need to*, I mean."

He smiled. "Only if you need to. And there is something else, Mary. Since you are my daughter, Fletcher Christian is your uncle. The Christian name is well known. And ever since your uncle Edward's book defending him, his name isn't so onerous anymore. The latest popular accounts hold Captain Bligh more than partially responsible for the mutiny. In some circles, the name of Fletcher Christian is assuming heroic proportions. And it's bound to come up for discussion in class, what with Coleridge's poem being so popular. So be careful."

"Sir?"

"Don't defend him, Mary. Or if you do, well, *just be careful not to bring suspicion upon yourself.* Do you understand?"

"Yes, sir."

He settled back into his seat and opened his newspaper. I thought he was finished speaking to me. I was beginning to be sorry I'd entered into any discussion. Uncle Charles stared at the front page of the newspaper for a moment; then, without looking at me, he said, "There is something else you should know, Mary."

I gave him my full attention.

He leaned toward Mr. Fettlestone first, to make sure he was sound asleep, then fastened his attention on me. "I was involved in a mutiny once. I thought you should know."

My mouth fell open. "You?"

"Yes. I was surgeon on the East Indiaman *Middlesex* back in 1787, under Captain John Rogers. We were bound for India, then Macao on the China coast. On the return voyage, we had trouble."

"What kind of trouble?"

He hesitated. My uncle Charles had a past.

Grandmother had said that he'd spent three years in the West Yorkshire militia, then gone to medical school in Edinburgh, and that he'd vowed to remain unmarried because, as a doctor, he was always convinced he was going to die within the next year. Grandmother had also said he'd always been pursued by women, most often rich women, and that he'd gone for a ship's surgeon to get away from one of them.

Even now, back home, there was talk that when lights glowed late in his cottage at night, there was a woman present. But we gave him his privacy.

"A ship can often be a place of much distress, Mary, with so many men confined for so long at sea. All the jarring peculiarities surface. Nerves are shattered. The best of men can give in to their evil tendencies. Captain Rogers put a man in irons, saying the man had put a pistol to his breast. Before it was over, four of us were locked up, and it was called mutiny. If it had been the navy, we could have been hanged from a yardarm, but it was private shipping. As it was, the East India Company censured us and suspended us from service for a couple of years. But the captain was seen as more than a little to blame."

I said nothing.

"But that's not the worst of it, Mary, and you should know this before we part. I met your father on that night you know of, when I was on the way home and he on the way out on the *Bounty*."

"Yes, sir. I've heard it."

"I told him of the mutiny. And I have blamed myself ever since. How do I know but that when his time came, he may have thought, Well, my brother Charles did this, and so why not me?"

"I don't think my father would think that, sir. He took responsibility for everything he did. You told me that."

"I blame myself nevertheless. I wanted you to know. And to know that it can so easily happen, a mutiny. And by good men."

"Thank you, Uncle Charles. I mean Papa."

He nodded and went back to his newspaper. The coach jogged along. A little later he said softly, "Beware of whom you speak, to whom, of what and where." Then he was reciting something:

> *"Give every man thine ear, but few thy*
> *   voice;*
> *Take each man's censure, but reserve*
> *   thy judgement."*

He looked at me. "That should be placed promi-
nently in every home, and on every ship, Mary.
Remember those words. Take them with you."

I nodded solemnly. He fascinated me, Uncle
Charles. I fancied that he had a lot of sadness and a lot
of secrets in him.

"Uncle Charles, I mean Papa, do you believe Gwen
about the fairies?"

"I think, as a physician, that she had a terribly
frightening experience up there on those rocks. Likely
she hallucinated. So she believes what she saw."

"Are there fairies and trolls and such, sir?"

He smiled. "As long as you choose to believe in
them, Mary."

And there was one more thing I needed to know.
"Have you seen my father since he brought me home?"
I whispered to Uncle Charles.

He looked at me, his eyes the color of the sea in a
storm. "Yes. So have you."

I felt as if I had been struck by thunder. "I?"

His eyes softened. "If you believe the stories that
he's been back, both of us may have seen him and not
known it. Do you think he would not be disguised
somehow in order to get about? It's like the fairies,
Mary. It's what you believe."

But there was something else here, *something I should know* and something he was not telling me. And he would speak no more.

I must have dozed off in the carriage, because I awoke to hear Uncle Charles saying, "We're in southeast London now. This is where we shall begin our tour."

I looked eagerly out the window and saw that we were crossing a bridge. "Is this the Thames?" I asked.

"Surely it is. The greatest waterway in the world. When it freezes, they hold frost fairs on the ice."

"Look at all those boats!"

"It's shallow here. The merchant ships dock down-river and the crewmen come up in wherries when the tide is good. There, can you see to the right? There is the Tower of London."

I looked. The White Tower rose in the distance like a fairy tale. People had been imprisoned in the Bloody Tower before being executed. "Will I see Execution Dock?" I asked. "Gwen says pirates are hanged there. And chained in place until three tides cover them."

"Gwen does come up with stories, doesn't she? No, you won't. Not while I'm with you."

But he pointed out everything to me as the coach made its way through the streets. "There, in the distance to the left, is St. Paul's Cathedral, the greatest

Protestant church in the world, Mary. It was rebuilt after the Great Fire in the seventeenth century. And a block north is Paternoster Row, where book publishers abound."

"Where does Uncle Edward live?"

"At Gray's Inn, where barristers live."

"Will he come visit me at school?"

"Only if you misbehave. Then I promise you he will be there. So I advise you not to misbehave."

Of a sudden, our coach came to a halt. The driver yelled, the horses gave a screeching whinny, and then we felt a thump as the driver jumped down.

"'Ere, what are you doin' there, you guttersnipe!"

"Oh, please, sir, I wuz just crossin' over."

"Crossin' in front, y'mean. Are you hurt?"

"I dunno, sir."

"Stay here," Uncle Charles said. Abruptly he opened the door and got out. I peered out the window. A small creature toting a sack, with a small dog beside him, was peering up at the driver, while people in carriages behind us shouted their impatience. *Creature* was the only word I could put on him. His face was covered with dirt, his hair lank and filthy, his clothes tattered. I saw Uncle Charles kneel down beside him, question him, feel his arms and legs, and then say something to the driver.

Mr. Fettlestone had awoken and was peering across the seat. "He isn't bringing that *thing* in here, is he?"

But Uncle Charles was. He'd picked up the *thing* and was carrying him to the carriage. I opened the door.

"You can't!" Mr. Fettlestone protested. "Dirt! Filth! Disease!"

"I can. He's hurt. We've run him down."

"If you bring him in here, I leave."

"Then leave," Uncle Charles said. He climbed inside the coach, carrying the boy. The boy's ragged little dog followed.

"Well, I never!" Mr. Fettlestone said. And he scrunched as close as he could to the other side of the carriage.

The boy looked to be no more then ten, a thin little fellow with the eyes of an old man. But he had the mouth of a Jack-tar. "Dirt, filth, disease yerself!" he shouted.

"Hush," Uncle Charles said sternly, "or I'll not help."

"Doan want yer bleedin' 'elp. Where's me sack?"

"You're not to bring a sack of rats in here," Uncle Charles said, closing the door firmly.

"Me sack! Me sack! I worked all mornin' to collect 'em. They're the best specimens I've seen in a dog's age. And where's me dog?"

"He's right here," Uncle Charles assured him. "But the rats aren't." Then he rapped the window, and the driver continued on. Uncle Charles had deposited the creature on the seat next to him and put me across the way, next to Mr. Fettlestone.

"A rat boy. You've got a rat boy," Mr. Fettlestone said.

"A what?" I asked.

He beamed at me, glad to be able to show his superior knowledge. "They collect rats for the sport."

"Sport?"

Uncle Charles had his doctor's bag opened and was attending to the boy, who was protesting loudly at having the blood wiped from his face. At his feet, his little dog barked and watched.

"They call it a sport," Mr. Fettlestone told me. "Ratting. They use terriers like that one there. Bet on them. Set them in rings with dozens of rats. It's illegal."

I shivered.

"Do it in cellars of public houses. Likely he's from St. Giles, where the gin-soaked live. They pit those little dogs against at least twenty-five rodents, and I'll wager the ones he had in his sack were from the river. The biggest."

"An' the best," the boy spat at him.

"And you were going to make your dog fight them?" I put the question to the boy himself.

"No. I just find the rats. An' deliver 'em to me master. He's the rat master. And now, thanks to 'im"—he gestured with his head at Uncle Charles—"I've lost me mornin's wages."

"I'll pay you for them," Uncle Charles said. "Your arm is broken. You must be attended to."

"Me arm?" The boy laughed.

"Doesn't it hurt?" Uncle Charles asked.

"Sure it do. But what don't? Me stomach hurts more when I'm hungry. Ye'll pay, you say?"

"Yes." Uncle Charles was busy looking at the arm.

"Well, the devil hisself will get me yet, if ye don't. 'Ow much?"

Uncle Charles reached into a pocket, and I heard coins clinking. "What are the rats worth?"

"Prime they is," the boy said. "The best. I know me rats. A bag like that? Five sovereigns."

Our fellow passenger gasped. "The fellow's a highway robber!"

"Shut yer trap," the boy shouted. Then he kicked Mr. Fettlestone, who yelled and held his shin.

"Enough!" Uncle Charles's voice was stern. He handed the boy the money, and we watched as the boy found an inside pocket in his ragged clothing and deposited it. "An' I ain't from bleedin' St. Giles!"

"Spitalfields, then, to judge from the vulgarity," Mr. Fettlestone said. "Or perhaps Moorfields or Bedlam."

Uncle Charles silenced them both and reached into his bag again.

Anybody could see the boy was in pain. "Me thanks for the King's shillin', but me master's dependin' on them rats fer tonight. Even if I give him what you give me, he'd be takin' the short of it. He makes a hunnert times that from bets."

"Well, he'll have to do without tonight. Your bones are smashed."

"To 'ell with me bones. He'll take me dog, Scully, if I don't deliver. An' I rescued Scully once from havin' to fight the rats. I ain't givin' him over agin."

"He won't take Scully, I promise." Uncle Charles drew a flask of something out of his bag and handed it to the boy.

"Thanks, mister," the boy said. And he greedily drank down greedily the contents of the flask.

"What's your name?" Uncle Charles asked.

"Willy's enough."

"All right, Willy, I'm going to get you fixed up."

"Don't need fixin'." And then Willy promptly nodded off.

We went on. We were in the heart of London now. "Unc—Papa, isn't it wonderful?"

Willy opened his eyes and looked at me intently. Had he heard me start to call my uncle "Uncle Charles" and not "Papa"?

"Fill your eyes, lass," Mr. Fettlestone said, "'Tis a lovely place, indeed. And like the good Lord Himself described heaven, there are many levels, from the abodes of the rich and the lavish shops and eateries to the people in the street—the lascars, the Chinese, the blackamoor seamen from North Africa and the Indies, the Irish scum; the bullies, pimps, footpads, river vultures, panderers, and all the rest of the riffraff."

Then he fell silent. I felt excitement mounting in me at the sights—the glass-fronted shops, the coffeehouses, the gentlemen's clubs, the fancy grocers and tea dealers, the flower markets, and the taverns that Uncle Charles pointed out to me. "In those fancy taverns, like The Devil and The Turk's Head, you'll likely find Charles Lamb or William Godwin," he said. Then he pointed out Fleet

Street as we passed onto it. "Over that way is Newgate Prison," he said.

Of course, to the left of us now was the Thames. All along it were the tall masts of ships, and on it were cargo boats, sailing boats, barges, ferries, even rowboats. At the next coach station Mr. Fettlestone got out, breathing heavily and casting angry looks at Uncle Charles. "Likely he's got malignant fever," he said of Willy. "Ah, Somerset House." He took off his hat, waved it at us, and said his farewells.

"What are you going to do with Willy?" I whispered to Uncle Charles as the coach lurched forward.

"Don't worry yourself. We'll be at your school soon. When we get there, just take things as they come. Let me attend to Willy."

My school was in St. James's Square, in an elegant part of town. The carriage stopped in front of a line of limestone houses, some with archways in front, some with giant pillars on the stories above us. All had large, sparkling windows, iron-filigree fences in front, and fall flowers in the narrow front gardens. In the middle of the square was a pond surrounded by trees and shrubs. The people walking around seemed to be eminent.

"Here we are," Uncle Charles said.

I shivered. There would be no setting snares for woodcock here, and I was ready to wager there wasn't a troll, good or bad, near the place. I looked up. Did I see people gazing down at us from the windows above our heads as we disembarked the coach? Staring as Uncle Charles carried out a sleeping urchin, a little rat terrier at his heels? What would they think of us?

The front door opened, and a man in smart breeches and a coat trimmed with red facing, which would have made him look like gentry at home, came to greet us.

"I'm Enfield, sir," he said. "I'm the underbutler. What have we here?"

"Our coach ran him down," Uncle Charles said. "I'm Dr. Christian, Mary's father, and I'd like a place to attend to the child. I'll pay."

Enfield nodded at me, summoned some servants, and consulted with a woman who had just come down the stairs.

"Greetings," she said. She did not curtsy. She extended her hand to Uncle Charles, who reached under Willy's body, which he was still holding, to grasp it.

I watched in amazement. Was this what blue-stockings did, then? Shook hands with men?

"I'm Sophia Hartsdale. I overheard you saying what happened to the child. Of course, you may come in and attend him. And we'll see what else can be done for him."

"He's a rat boy," Uncle Charles said. "Looks like he hasn't bathed for a year. I don't think he has any diseases, though. No fever. Just needs cleaning up."

"This way, sir," said Enfield.

Miss Hartsdale turned to me. She was wearing a blue dress of a plainness that bespoke gentility. Her hair was done primly in a bun, with some curls hanging over her ears. Her eyes were friendly, her teeth perfect, and her manner matched, as her shoes matched her dress.

"Welcome, welcome, welcome, dear child!" she said. "Do come in."

⌒ SEVEN

And so it was that I arrived at the Misses Hartsdale's School for Young Ladies. I must write to Gwen, I decided. She would never believe this. A *rat boy*! Wasn't that better than a troll or a fairy or a hobgoblin?

Inside the dazzling entryway, a chandelier hung overhead, and busts of women I did not recognize sat on marble stands. A curved stairway made a sweeping bow. And there were girls on it, three of them. All dressed in the same blue as Miss Sophia, all wearing different hairdos. Maids fluttered about. My hamper and trunk were taken up the stairs. Immediately, all the girls gathered around Uncle Charles and oohed and aahed at Willy.

"Stay away," Uncle Charles said. "Don't frighten him. Miss Sophia, direct me."

"Certainly. Rawlings?" she called out, and another butler appeared, only this one had gold on his uniform, which even I knew designated him as above all the other servants. His long, upturned nose, bald head, and white gloves told me that, if his superior attitude didn't.

"Certainly, Miss Sophia. Come along, sir."

He and Uncle Charles disappeared through an arch down a hallway, followed by Miss Sophia. I could tell that she was already taken with Uncle Charles. Most women were.

Now I was left to be stared at. By three girls.

"Is it damp outside?" I was asked.

And "Did you see the orange girl in the square? She's got scarlet strawberries, too. We buy from her every day, but we're being punished today. We can't go out."

"Why?" I asked.

"Because we tied a rope around a bust of William Cowper and lowered it out the front third-story window."

"William Cowper?" I thanked heaven for Grandmother's teaching. "Don't you like him?"

"Yes," one girl said, "but his poetry elaborates a vision of feminine sensibility as victimhood, which we don't care for."

"I see." I looked around me. Was there a way out? I could see immediately that I would come to be regarded here as we regarded the fabled three-headed giant on Man.

They were staring at me, waiting for an answer. A clever one. And I knew then that this was a gauntlet I must run. I thought fast.

"I prefer Jean-Jacques Rousseau," I said. "His republican advocacy of simplicity of manners against aristocratic corruption made him a hero in liberal middle class circles." Thank heaven for Uncle Charles. He was always spouting off about Rousseau.

"You're a Christian," the tallest girl said. She was very fair in color. "You're not middle class."

"You're from the Isle of Man," said the second. She wore dark ringlets and was about thirteen. "I've heard it's magical there. Is it?"

Here was my forte, then. I would tell of Man's magic, and thank Gwen every night in my prayers. "Yes," I said. "We have mermaids, fairies, hobgoblins, everything. But although my family were rulers over the last six hundred years and my father's grandfather was Queen Anne's solicitor, we are now middle class. My grandmother runs a lodging house."

More staring. Then another girl came into the entry-way, carrying a large black and white cat. "What's all the excitement?" she asked.

"The *new girl*," the tallest girl said. And there was contempt in the words.

"Who is the boy?" The girl with the cat came over to me. "I'm Fanny. And this is Jane," she said, pointing to the tall, fair girl. "Celeste here, with the lovely dark ringlets, and Alice. I hope you girls aren't being harsh on our newcomer."

"Thank you," I said, "but they weren't. They were, as a matter of fact, being kind." I sensed Fanny must be the oldest, and as such had some sort of authority over the others. "And the boy is an urchin we ran down with our coach. My father is seeing to him."

"Your father is a doctor," Fanny said.

"Yes."

"Didn't your mother tell you to stay out of the sun?" Alice asked.

"Alice!" Fanny scolded.

"It's all right." I sighed. Might as well get it over with. "I was born in the West Indies," I said. "When my father was a ship's surgeon."

"Ohhh, how *romantic*!" Jane sighed.

"Yes," I agreed.

Fanny stepped forward and touched my face lightly. "I love your complexion. You look so alive."

"I think I was touched by a mermaid," I said. I don't know what made me say it, except that I knew it would enhance me in their eyes. I sensed immediately that in spite of their curls and satin slippers, their silk dresses and perfect manners, they were like Gwen. They needed fantasy. They were hungry for it.

"This is Dick Turpin," Fanny said of the cat in her arms.

I petted him. I like cats. Uncle Charles had one living with him, a big red one, and it slept on his bed.

"He's named after the famous highwayman who was hanged in 1739. He steals every bit of food in the house that he can get his claws on," Jane said.

"He's beautiful," I said.

"Did you know that Turpin broke into houses to steal, and once, when an old woman wouldn't tell where she hid her money, he sat her on the fire until she told?" asked Alice.

"I expect she told right quick," I said.

"And he murdered people in Essex," Celeste said.

"Then why name your cat after him?" I asked Fanny.

"Oh, he's not mine. He belongs to Lizzy, who's having an art lesson across the square with Phillipa Reynolds. She's the sister of the great artist. We all go for lessons. And if Lizzy saw me even *holding* Dick Turpin, she'd scratch my eyes out. But she named him that because Turpin had himself made a fancy coat and new boots to be hanged in. And this Turpin has a fancy black and white fur coat, too."

At that moment another lady came into the entryway. She was short and dumpy and downright ugly, with a too-large nose and graying hair worn in a bun. And her eyebrows met in the middle. But her eyes seemed to have a mischievous twinkle. "You must be frazzled after your long journey. Alice, go into the kitchen and ask Dorothy to bring up a tray of tea for Mary. The rest of you"—and she clapped her hands—"scat, now, upstairs, all of you!"

They ran away, and I was about to follow, but the lady's hand on my arm stayed me. "I'm Miss Harriet. I know I don't look like my sister. She's the pretty one. But we're twins, only I was born first and got spanked in the face by the midwife. That's why I'm ugly."

"You're not ugly," I lied.

"Sweet of you. Now, if you go up the winding

stairway and down another hall, you'll be met by a giant who'll say 'Fe, fi, fo, fum.' No"—and she laughed—"Dorothy will show you to your room. You're lucky and unlucky. Lucky because your room is in front and overlooks the square. Unlucky because you room with Lizzy."

"The girl who owns the cat?"

"Yes. Try being nice. If that doesn't work, heaven help you. Go."

I went with Dorothy. Upstairs, the other girls were waiting for me in front of my room. It was large, with a high ceiling, gauzy curtains, tall bedsteads, dark wainscoting, and Persian carpets. Never had I seen such a room. French doors opened onto a tiny terrace. "I envy you so," Fanny sighed. "I'd take my morning tea out there."

Another maid was unpacking my things. While she did so, the girls sat on one of the beds and sat me down on it, too. Soon my tea was brought, and it was as if I'd been there for a week already.

When I thanked the maid, she bobbed a curtsy. "I'm Callie, miss. From Ireland."

"Thank you, Callie from Ireland," I said.

"We don't make friends of maids," said Celeste solemnly. "We must mind our class distinctions."

"Don't mind her." Fanny pushed Celeste gently. "She's French. Leastways, she was born there. Her mother was carrying her while she watched her husband get his head chopped off in their revolution."

"Not true!" Tears came to Celeste's eyes.

"Come now, Celeste," Fanny said patiently. "You know we all have hidden backgrounds here. And guessing whether they're true or not, that is part of the game we play. Because if they are true, people think it's a game. And if they aren't, nobody is hurt." She flashed a beautiful smile at me. "And we all agree that no one must ever be pushed to tell the truth about her past," she said.

Past? Could young girls have a past? Well, I did, didn't I? And then, as if she had read my mind, Fanny said, "And not even you have to tell us of yours if you don't want to."

"Although we all know about you," Celeste added.

My heart pounded inside. "What?"

"Your uncle Fletcher did a mutiny. He's famous."

I felt myself flush from head to toe.

"They say he's back in England, you know." This from Jane.

"Who?"

"Your uncle Fletcher. Didn't you know that?"

I shook my head no, remembering Uncle Charles's recitation. *Beware of whom you speak, to whom, of what and where.*

"It was in the papers. A man named Heywood said he saw him on Fore Street by Plymouth Dock just a month ago."

Heywood. *Where had I heard that name?*

I stretched my memory way back, but could not place it. Hadn't a man named Heywood come around to see Grandmother one night a few years back?

The room seemed to sway for a moment. I shrugged. *Give every man thine ear, but few thy voice.*

"Do you think he'll come see you?" Fanny asked.

"Does he even know you're here?" This from Jane.

"When did you last see him? Ever?" From Celeste.

"We're studying all about him." From Alice.

Miss Harriet came in then, thank heaven. "Who?" she asked.

"Why, Fletcher Christian! He's her uncle!" As the oldest, Fanny had no fear.

"Well, don't embarrass Mary now. Not on her first day here!" Miss Harriet said. "Wait until the second day at least. And yes, we are studying him, Mary. More precisely, we are studying Mr. Coleridge's poem about him. But we won't, if it pains you."

"Oh, I love the poem," I said. "Please don't stop on my account."

"Good girl." She smiled. "You have a water closet, Mary, did the girls tell you?" And she walked across the hall and opened a door and gestured. "A sink with running water. A copper tub. And a necessary. Isn't mankind ingenious? I would advise you not to drink the water right after it gets pumped in."

"Or ever," Celeste said.

"Mankind hasn't been ingenious enough yet to filter it. Water gets pumped in three times a week," Miss Harriet went on. "Then you are welcome to ask the maid to heat some and fill the tub for you so you can bathe."

"Thank you," I said. Thank heaven, I thought. No more going out back to the necessary.

"Mary has been traveling for two days, and now I want her to go downstairs to say good-bye to her father and then nap before supper, girls," Miss Harriet said.

One by one they got up and reluctantly left. All except Alice. She stayed long enough to whisper to me, "My father is Jack Ketch. He is the executioner at Newgate."

Then she was gone, and I was left alone for a

moment in the elegant room with my tea and Dick Turpin.

I found Uncle Charles, Miss Sophia, and Willy in a small, sunny room off the kitchen. Willy was ensconced on a small bed, covered with a quilt, his head and arm bandaged. He'd been bathed and wore a clean nightshirt.

"We'll show you where you can wash," Miss Sophia told Uncle Charles. She directed him through the kitchen, and he disappeared behind a door.

"They're gonna keep me 'ere like I wuz an invalid," Willy complained to me. "They took Scully an' they're washin' him. Could you go see? An' make sure they ain't killin' him, too?"

"Of course," I said.

I saw, right off, that Callie was washing Scully in a bucket out on the back terrace. "He's a little terror," she said, smiling at me. "Would you like to pour that pot of warm water there over him, please, while I hold him down?"

I did so. Scully's fur went straight under the assault of water. Afterward, he shook his body, and water spattered in all directions. I backed off. Callie got wet. "The towel!" she cried. "Quick!"

I fetched it from the ground and watched Callie rub the dog dry. He looked unhappy, but he smelled clean. Once released, he ran around in circles. "He's gone daft," Callie said dismally.

"No, he's happy to be clean. My papa has a dog at home who does that after a bath, too."

"We're glad to have you here, Miss Christian," Callie said. She wrung out the towel with strong hands. "You seem like a good addition. Sensible. And not spoiled. Just too bad they put you in with that Lizzy. Well"—she sighed—"I suppose the misses have their reasons. But be careful. She thinks herself a fancy lady, that one."

"A *fancy lady*?"

"No, not like that. I mean, she says she's going to marry a marquess. Or a lord. Always getting permission to go off to assemblies and the like. Always gadding about. And whatever you do, don't touch her cat. You'd better run now. I see your father waving. And take the dog, will you?"

I picked up Scully, who was all but dry, and carried him back inside. Uncle Charles smiled as I put him down on the bed next to Willy. I waited as Uncle Charles gave Miss Sophia instructions as to Willy's medicine and care and then left some money on a small table.

"I'll send a doctor around to see him until he recovers," he promised.

Then he walked me out. "Visit Willy when you can," he said.

"Yes, sir. But what will happen to him?"

"Maybe I could bring him home. We could use a smart lad about the place to run errands for your grandmother."

"Uncle Charles, Grandmother told you not to bring home any more strays."

He smiled. "Don't worry the matter. You've enough to worry about, getting settled here." Then he gave me a small sack of coins. "For shopping," he said.

I hugged him, feeling the tears well in my eyes.

"Be a good girl, now. And write," he admonished me.

"Uncle Charles . . ." But I could think of nothing to say.

He went out the front door. "I've errands to run before I start back. I'm meeting my brother Edward tonight for supper. You'll like it here, Mary. I promise."

Then he was gone.

EIGHT

Dinner was at three o'clock in the girls' dining room.
There was a larger, more formal one for visitors. Ours
was surrounded by small-paned windows that looked
out on the flower garden. Everything was blue and
white, even the china.

"They leave us our own room to talk in," said Fanny.
"As the oldest, I'm to say grace."

She did so, handsomely, and then we ate—pea soup,
a boiled rump of beef, chopped spinach, figs, and bat-
ter custard pudding. It was all very good.

All the while, Dick Turpin lay curled up at my feet.

"He's taken a fancy to you," Jane said. "You're lucky
Lizzy isn't here."

"Where is she?"

"After her lessons, she takes the Queen's Walk in St. James's Park. We missed it today because of your arrival. She's with Miss Reynolds. The walk is usually from twelve to two, but on nice days they sometimes linger. All the elite hereabouts attend. When you go with us, remember to wear your best bonnet."

I knew I would never walk on my own in London. At home, when we walked, it was to go somewhere. "Who are Lizzy's people?" I asked.

Fanny smiled. "She says she's the daughter of Charles Lamb."

We waited until Enfield and Callie left the room.

"Is she?" I asked.

Jane shrugged. "You know, Charles Lamb writes children's books. Well, Lizzy says, his sister, Mary Lamb, *really wrote some of them*. She's quite insane now, though. But Lizzy seems to know what she's saying. Then again, it could just be her pretend family. Though all these famous people have illegitimate children. It's the thing to do. Little Sibella over there, do you know who she is?"

Sibella was fair and round-faced, and very pretty. About nine. "Real or pretend?" I asked.

"Does it matter? She says she's the illegitimate

daughter of Lady Emma Hamilton and Lord Nelson. Do you remember what a scandal their affair was?"

"My grandmother doesn't hold with gossip, but yes, I know."

"Lady Hamilton met Nelson in Naples in 1793. He's dead now. But Sibella's mother put her here at age two. Just as Lizzy's mother did. And scarcely ever comes to see her."

"Does she speak often of her father?"

"It's just *known*," Jane said. "You don't talk about your background, do you?"

I held my tongue.

"Cheer up and don't look like a naughty child. We love you already," Jane said. "And upstairs we're going to sing for you later."

I looked around at the girls at the table. There were only five here, including myself. A small school in a large house. Then why did they put two in a room?

"Miss Sophia and Miss Harriet want you to look after each other," someone said. It was Callie. I hadn't noticed, but she had slipped back into the room to serve tea, and whispered it over my shoulder. I stared at her. Was it an innocent statement? Or did she read minds?

Callie met my eyes and smiled. And I knew then. She read minds.

"We have our Morals and Philosophy class this afternoon," Fanny put in. "So hurry up with your tea. You'll like the class, I promise."

Morals and Philosophy turned out to be a sort of discussion free-for-all bound together by Miss Harriet, who soon became unbound.

This day the topic was "What Books Not to Read as a Thinking, Intellectual Young Woman." That alone set me back. In a school such as this, I would have thought the only book not to read would be called *The Devil's Handbook*, or something with a similar name. But I was wrong.

"Tell me one book we should never waste time on," said Miss Harriet.

Lizzy had finally decided to honor us with her presence. She came in late, breathless, rosy-cheeked and beautiful, with luxuriant hair the color of rust, a pert nose and chin, strong cheekbones, and a smile that flashed the whitest of teeth.

"Oh, Miss Harriet, I have a question for you."

"Yes?" Miss Harriet looked up.

"I must have a holiday, Miss Harriet."

"A holiday?" Miss Harriet's curious eyebrows went up. "We've just started the school year, Lizzy."

"Well, it's more of a family emergency, ma'am."

"Is your mother ill?"

"No. My father is writing a new children's book. Called *Mrs. Leicester's School*. And he's asked me to cast a schoolgirl's eye on it. You know, my aunt is no longer able to help him. She's gone quite insane since she killed my grandmother twelve years ago."

Some of the girls oohed and aahed, as I suppose we were all meant to do. Lizzy stood there, then dramatically swept her velvet cape off her shoulders and set it aside. "My father needs me, ma'am."

Miss Harriet sighed. A moment passed in which the pale daytime moon outside went and hid itself behind a cloud in shame. And we all waited to see if Miss Harriet would agree to this charade. Or acknowledge it to be a charade, but give permission anyway.

"I'll discuss it with my sister and see," she said. "Now sit down, please."

Lizzy sat. Then she spoke again. "In answer to your question, ma'am, one book we should not read is *An Enquiry into the Duties of the Female Sex*, by Thomas Gisborne."

"And why not?" Miss Harriet asked.

"Because," Lizzy answered, "it discourages alliances of commonality across the ranks of women."

"Excellent!" Miss Harriet clapped her hands. "Any other books?"

"There are few novels that can be read with safety," Lizzy went on. "If a woman reads unsuitable novels, she is prostituting her soul."

And what if she lies about who her father is? I asked myself. What if? Isn't that what I do? And perhaps this girl has as good a reason.

"At home I read everything," I burst out.

"Everything?" Miss Harriet asked.

"Yes, ma'am. My papa allows me freedom in his library. Of course they are mostly medical books, but he's got some fine novels and biographies and poetry there, too."

"I'm sure he does," Miss Harriet agreed, "but in this school, we're concerned with the moral and intellectual self-discipline of the female reader."

"I read when I want to get away from the world," I said. "Sometimes I take a book to a secluded glen and read the afternoon away."

"You read for enjoyment," Miss Harriet said. "There is no harm in that. Except that now, at your age, all your reading should be for self-improvement and intellectual growth."

I wasn't hearing her. I was back behind our house

and barn, in a glen by the brook, reading. Across the way from me there was a shadow in the bushes, made by what? A deer? Or my father, watching me?

"Of course, I'm always on the lookout for trolls," I said.

I don't know what made me say it, but I wanted to be back in that glen and not here in a swamp of intellectual superiority. I hated intellectual superiority. It was what Uncle Edward was afflicted with.

"Trolls?" Miss Harriet asked.

There, I'd done it now. Well, good. Were trolls any worse to speak of than lying about Charles Lamb being your father? What angered me here was that all these girls made up glamorous backgrounds, adventurous and romantic fathers. And I had one, and I couldn't admit to it.

"Yes, ma'am, trolls. I look for them for my friend Gwen. I mean our maid. She's always looking for trolls. Why, right before I came here, she was lost for four days on the rocks near Pigeon Stream, two hundred feet above sea level. Just because she was trying to find a good troll to bring her luck."

"Oh, I read about that in *The Morning Post*," Jane cried. "The girl on the rocks! We all read about that. That's Gwen, your maid?"

"Yes," I said proudly. "But we didn't know it was in the papers."

"We're supposed to be reading *The Times*," Miss Harriet said.

"It was such a romantic account," Jane said. "I have a copy, if you wish. You can send it to Gwen."

"Oh, thank you. That would be lovely."

There were evening prayers in the front parlor. Miss Harriet and Miss Sophia read literary parts of the Bible. We sat on small gold-and-white chairs in a room lighted with candles. Then Miss Sophia spoke of the day's events, garnering lessons from them.

On my lap sat Dick Turpin.

Miss Sophia went over the business of Willy, lying in his small room. "A rat boy," she said in a reverent whisper. "Do you girls even realize what sort of lives some of the children on London's streets live? Dr. Christian said the boy likely hadn't bathed in a year, and likely slept on a pile of rags in some cellar. Now, you all know, girls, that my sister and I have decided that for this school year we are going to do some charity work. And so are you. So let's mull over the matter a bit and come up with some suggestions, why don't we?"

Everybody thought for a moment, but before

anybody could speak, Lizzy made her entrance. And it could be called only that.

She pulled one of the satin ribbons of her darling bonnet, removed it, and shook a head full of glistening curls. "Oh, the concert was heavenly," she said, doing a small dance. "And you'll never guess who I was introduced to this night! Maria Edgeworth, the novelist. She sends her regards!"

"Did you invite her to come visit?" Miss Sophia asked.

"Of course. But she was with people! Oh, I wish I had her book so she could sign it for me!" Then she stopped twirling and spied me.

"What is she doing with my cat on her lap?"

"Now, don't be rude, Lizzy," Miss Sophia said.

But Lizzy had every intention of being rude. She marched around the array of gold-and-white chairs and stood next to me. But it was not me to whom she spoke.

"Dick Turpin, what are you about?" she said sternly.

The cat was purring. He looked up at her and blinked.

She reached down and took him from me. "Naughty boy, going to strangers! What did I tell you about that?" she cooed. Then: "Please, may I be excused from meditations?"

"Don't you want to know about Willy, the rat boy, whom we've taken under our wing?" Fanny asked.

But Lizzy went to the door. "The last one you brought in was a sweeping boy who'd gotten burned in a chimney. May I be excused?"

"You are sharing the room with Mary," Miss Sophia said.

"Well, one can't be choosy, can one?" And with that she walked out.

"I'm sorry, Mary," Miss Sophia said. "She is a little strange. Be patient with her, will you?"

"It's all right," I said. But somehow I knew it would not be.

Later, upstairs, the girls all got into nightdresses and visited back and forth between rooms. They told stories and lies, repeated gossip, and handed about treats. When I went to my room to change, I saw that Lizzy was already in her nightdress, on her bed reading, with Dick Turpin beside her.

Behind a curtain, I changed into my nightdress. "If you touch my cat again, you'll be sorry," came Lizzy's voice in a normal, everyday tone.

I gathered my clothes and set them on a chair. "He seeks me out," I said.

"He cares for no one but me."

"Whatever you choose to think," I said.

She looked at me. "You're a Christian, aren't you?"

"Yes, but I'm not a fist-pounding Methodist."

"Don't be snide. You know what I mean. You're from that family who was disgraced because of the *Bounty* affair."

"According to what I've learned already here today, disgrace is a kind of virtue. All the girls have invented secret identities that have to do with murky backgrounds."

"Mine isn't invented. But being the illegitimate daughter of Charles Lamb is a sight better than being the daughter of the man who turned against King and country."

"I'm not his daughter. I'm his niece."

"It's all the same thing. Let me tell you right now, Mary Christian, if you go flaunting that around here, you'll be sorry. Yes, the girls have invented secret backgrounds. Do you know why? To compete with me. *Because mine is real.* They've made it into a game. Yours is real, too. But a disgrace. Everybody knows that. So don't boast of who you are. It's nothing to boast of."

"I don't speak of it," I said.

"Good." She went back to her reading.

"Anything else?" I asked.

"Yes. This is my room. You are a guest. And I've lived here since I was two, so I am considered with respect. Remember that, Mary Christian."

I said I would, and went to join the others.

That night, before I went to bed, I put on a wrap and asked permission to visit Willy. Miss Sophia came with me.

"If anythin' 'appens to me, would you take care of Scully?" he asked me. The room was dark. I could scarcely see his face.

"Why should anything happen to you? My father said you'd be fine."

Miss Sophia was summoned by her sister and left the room. Willy winked at me. "I 'eard you callin' 'im Uncle."

I flushed. "It was a mistake. Some of his little patients call him that."

"Mistake, hey? I 'eard who you be. And 'im. Does it mean you're the daughter, then? You're the right color."

I bit my lower lip.

"Look, miss, I ain't bein' disrespectful or nuthin'. We all got our problems, an' mine is bigger than any. Yer secret's safe with me."

Somehow I knew it would be. And somehow I knew
Willy was using his promise as currency to get what he
wanted from me. And I was right.

"Miss," he said, "I gots to get outa 'ere. Else the rat
master is gonna find me and slit me throat fer not
bringin' round the rats tonight. He depends on them.
An' me."

"He won't find you," I said.

He laughed, then winced, because it hurt to laugh.
"You doan know 'im like I does. He could find a speck
of dust in a witch's eye. Listen now. It ain't only me I'm
worried 'bout. He'll come 'ere, rob the place maybe.
But worst, he'll take me dog and put 'im in the pit.
Scully wuz in the pit once. A real fighter, 'e wuz. But
'e got bit and near died, and I gave me services free for
six months to take 'im away from all that."

I just stared at the undersized figure in the bed,
bandaged and with eyes so old, they might belong to a
grandfather.

"What do you want from me?" I asked.

"I'm sneakin' out tonight. I'm leavin' Scully. Just
look after him. I'll be back. I gots to pay the rat master
for tonight's catch."

"All right," I promised. "But take care of yourself."

I slept fitfully that night. The house fell silent, but it creaked, like all old houses. I dozed and woke half a dozen times to hear footsteps in the hall or on the stairs. Lizzy snored. I heard the water pumping in through the iron pipes, and knew all the girls would be in line for baths tomorrow. Outside, on the cobblestone street, I head the clopping of the horse pulling the cart of the man who put out the oil lamps around midnight.

I heard talk from the street, and a flaring kind of light flashed across the walls of my room. And I knew it was some linkboys carrying torches, hired to see late fun seekers home.

Then, when the tall case clock chimed midnight, I heard something slam downstairs.

Willy. Gone out a window. I shivered.

Then I felt something warm and furry next to my head in the bed. And I heard purring. Dick Turpin licked my nose and settled down next to me for the night, and I slept.

⌐ NINE

I awoke next morning to screams and slaps. I had been dreaming again of being in a cabin on a boat. Then a door burst open, and an angry mermaid broke in and attacked me.

As it turned out, that angry mermaid was Lizzy.

"What are you doing with my cat?"

She was pulling my hair. Dick Turpin jumped off the bed. I struggled to get up, couldn't, and decided to roll over to protect my face, which she had already scratched.

I kicked and screamed, but she was on top of me. Then I bit her arm and she yelled as if seven fairies were about to kidnap her: "Oh, oh, I'm bleeding! Oh, she bit me!"

"Girls! What is this?" Miss Sophia stood there, all prim and crisp in her morning dress. "Shame! For shame! Stand back, both of you!"

I struggled to stand at all, then took my place beside Lizzy. Both of us looked like fishwives. Miss Sophia demanded an explanation. Of course, Lizzy gave one.

"She took my cat. And when I politely asked for his return, she responded with the most terrible curses and slaps. I had to defend myself."

"Mary?" I was asked.

"The cat came to me. And she slapped me first."

"I'm ashamed of both of you. Mary, what would your father say? And as if to add to our miseries this morning, Willy has absconded and left us with his ragged little dog."

"Willy? Gone?" But why was I surprised? I'd known it last night.

"Mary, I'm afraid I have to send a note around to your uncle Edward," Miss Sophia said. "Lizzy, I'm sending a note to your father, too."

"Uncle Edward? Why?" I asked.

"Because I won't fetch your father back from

wherever he is. Likely he's on a stagecoach this very minute, bound for home. And the name I was given for an emergency was your uncle Edward's. He's a barrister, is he not?"

No, I wanted to say. He's a dependable snob and stuffy dull wit.

"I shall send a note around. And he will visit. Now, get dressed. There will be no walk in St. James's Park for either of you today."

I would rather have been strung on a yardarm than have Uncle Edward visit. I longed to be outside. I missed my romps in and around Douglas. But I obeyed, with a sinking heart. Uncle Edward!

Uncle Edward came around teatime. I was summoned from tea by Miss Sophia and taken to the front parlor, where he sat before a fire because it was raining outside. His blue barrister's bag sat on the floor next to him.

He wore a double-breasted coat of the finest worsted, a waistcoat, and a stand-up collar and cravat. His breeches were fawn-colored, and his white silk hose were spotless. I knew he prided himself on his well-formed calves. I knew, too, that he used jasmine butter for his hair, and perfumed mouth water, because

I'd poked about in his things one time when he came to visit Grandmother.

I curtsied. "Hello, Uncle Edward."

He stood, being forever the gentleman. His eyes went over my form and obviously approved the flowing sky-blue high-waisted dress with the scoop neck and long sleeves. "So, one day here and I'm summoned already."

He bowed as Miss Sophia left the room, then sat down again. Callie brought him a tray of tea and cakes.

When she had left, he turned to me. "Sit. Do you wish some tea?"

"No, thank you, sir."

"Well, what have you to say for yourself?"

I rushed forward to serve his tea for him, as I'd been taught. He took it and gestured that I must sit. I did, opposite him.

"It wasn't my fault, sir. She attacked me because her cat has taken a liking to me and she's jealous."

"Of what?" His eyes narrowed.

I knew he was waiting for me to say "Because I'm a Christian, and my family goes back six hundred years." But I did not. "Because her cat favors me."

He harrumphed. "Did you tell Miss Sophia that?"

"Yes, sir. But Lizzy's story was better. Mine didn't

stand up by comparison. It sounded stupid."

"The truth is never stupid, if it is the truth." He sounded as if he were in a courtroom. "Did you bite her?"

I knew better than to lie to Uncle Edward. His eye was sharper than the Almighty's. Besides, I'd earned myself the only spanking I ever had as a child for lying to him. "Yes, sir."

"Biting is done by the lower classes. Do you wish to be like the fishwives?"

"No, sir."

"Did she scratch your face like that?"

"Yes, sir.

He sipped his tea. "I used to teach at Hawkshead Grammar School, you know. When Wordsworth was there. Many's the thrashing I gave that young man, and if you and this—what's her name?"

"Lizzy, sir. She says her father is Charles Lamb."

"Does she? Nevertheless, if you and Lizzy were in my class at Hawkshead, you'd both receive a proper thrashing."

"Girls don't go there, sir."

"Are you being saucy to me?"

"No, sir, sorry. I didn't intend such."

"Then what do you intend, Mary Christian? To learn something here to redeem yourself? Or to be a guttersnipe?"

"To learn, sir, surely."

"Well, if I'm summoned again, I shall take you out of here and send you home to earn threepence a day for spinning. Is that understood?"

"Yes, sir."

He set down his cup. "Go and fetch Miss Sophia. No, wait."

I paused at the doorway.

"What's this about my brother bringing a rat boy here for care and his running off?"

"I don't know any more than he told me, sir. And what he told me was that he had to bring his earnings for last night's losses to his master, or his master would take his little dog and put him back in the pits."

"He told you he was running off, and you didn't report it?"

"Sir, he said if he didn't bring his earnings and turn them over, the man would come here and slash his throat. And endanger all of us."

"Nevertheless, you should have reported it. These

good ladies were responsible for him."

I could not think what *these good ladies* would do if Willy's master came around to slash his throat. But I said, "Yes, sir," and went to fetch Miss Sophia. I'm not stupid.

"I insist Mary be punished for her behavior and for biting Lizzy's arm," Uncle Edward told Miss Sophia when we returned.

Miss Sophia looked as if she would rather face a three-headed giant than Uncle Edward. "I'm afraid they're both to blame, Mr. Christian," she said.

"I'm not concerned with the other girl. Consult Charles Lamb about her. I'm concerned with my niece's paying for her actions. What do you suggest?"

"No tea for a week?" Miss Sophia smiled prettily.

Uncle Edward scowled.

"Well, then." Miss Sophia's shoulders slumped. She was defeated. "For cursing, I'm afraid I resort to the old remedy of washing their mouths out with soap. Either that or spending a night alone in the laundry room. But I cannot do either of those things to Mary. She's a sweet child."

"Then get me some soap and show me the way to the kitchen," he ordered her.

Now Miss Sophia was truly distressed. She put both hands over her face and cried. I went to her. "Ma'am? It's all right, truly. I don't mind. Uncle Edward has done it to me before."

I sat her down by the fire and poured her some tea, and showed Uncle Edward to the kitchen. The maids, who obviously had been listening, ran when they saw him. He put down his blue barrister's bag, took off his waistcoat, loosened his cuffs, and rolled them up. Then he reached for the soap.

"Sir, I just want to say that I'll take the punishment so you'll know I'm speaking the truth now. But I didn't curse."

He scowled. "Open your mouth."

I did so. I squeezed my eyes shut. Next thing I knew, some foul-smelling and nasty soap, tasting as if it were made of lard—which it likely was—was generously smeared inside my mouth.

Uncle Edward stopped when I commenced choking. I bent over the basin, ready to throw up. "Drink some water," he said. "Wash your mouth out. It needs washing." Then he grabbed up his waistcoat and blue barrister's bag and left.

I heard the front door slam. Miss Sophia came into the kitchen, distraught and apologetic. "I shouldn't have called for him, Mary. I'm sorry; I didn't know."

She helped me. When I was able to speak again, I said, "He says I'm the perfect example of original sin."

"Dear, men always think such of women. The woman is always blamed. Oafish husbands can use a stick to beat their wives as long as it's no bigger in circumference than a thumb. But you don't need to hear of this now. Come, let's have us a nice quiet cup of tea, and we'll talk about how to get Willy back."

Then she hugged me. And we had our tea and became friends for life.

And Willy came back the very next day.

I was the first to see him. We were in the garden for our evening walk. The rain had stopped, the pale moon was rising, everything was shiny and clean, and I was walking Scully. I should say that it was Scully who first heard him, and the dog ran to the garden gate.

Willy had on the old clothes he had been brought in. And he looked as if someone had beaten him. He had a swollen purple mark on his forehead, a cut lip, and a swollen left eye, and he limped.

"Willy!" I ran to the gate.

"'Ello, miss."

"Where have you been?"

"I brought the money me master lost from the other night."

"The money my father gave you?"

"That's it."

"But who beat you?"

"Me master. Who else? Then he wanted me to stay, but I run again. He says next time 'e'll kill me."

"Oh, do come in! We've been so worried!"

Willy was on his knees, patting Scully, who was licking his injured face. He picked up Scully and carried him through the garden in his arms. "Is it awright? Ain't they bloomin' mad at me?"

"Just worried. Here, come into your room in the back. I'll ask Callie to fetch some water and your other clothing."

Before I left, he clutched my sleeve. "Miss Mary, there's somethin' I should tell you."

"Yes?"

"A person who knows you wants to come and visit."

"Who?" My brain raced. Did he mean Langston? Had he somehow met Langston?

"His name is Peter 'Eywood."

Thunder sounded. A storm was coming. I felt the wind out of the east. I looked around. What wind?

There was none. It was inside my head.

"I think I know that name," I said carefully.

"Course you do. He served on the *Bounty* with your father."

Peter Heywood! Why could I not put a face to that name?

"How did you meet him?"

"I knows a lot of people in an' around the docks here in London, miss. But he comes from Man. He was fourteen when he signed on to the *Bounty*."

"What do you know of it all?"

"No more than anybody else what's 'eard of it. And that this Mr. 'Eywood wants to see you. I kin give 'im a message, if you say yes."

I stood, trembling.

He looked up at me with one battered eye. Just then, Callie and Miss Harriet came through the door. Callie had a basin of hot water, and clean rags and soap. She passed swiftly by me, stood in front of Willy, and said, "Take off your shirt, young man. I know you've got bruises on your back."

Miss Harriet leaned close to me and said, "Let him come."

How had she heard? She hadn't, I decided. She just knew.

I nodded at her and ran from the room.

The night after the fight with Lizzy, I had gone to bed in a different room. It was smaller, but decorated crisply in yellow and white. It looked down on the square.

I was happy to be there. I set down my things and surveyed my privacy.

"There's no bad serpent that doesn't drag good on its tail," Grandmother always said. "That's why they swish their tails so. Trying to get the good off."

Everyone was surprised at Willy's return. Miss Sophia asked him to stay.

"You can do errands. And we need a boy in the stables to care for the horses."

He stayed. They bought him some shiny, black

boots and sets of clothing, and when his hair was cut he was downright handsome.

He told me, on the sly, that the work would be easy. His parents had sold him to his master for ten shillings five years ago. I could scarcely believe it. He was but twelve. He knew everything about the streets of London—how to take shortcuts, which people to avoid. He said there were many children on London's streets just like him.

Miss Harriet and Miss Sophia paid him, too. He ran errands for them, and even for the butlers. "The poor fare hard," Miss Harriet said.

"Still, me problems ain't over," he told me. "I'd wager me master will try to find me dog. He's a good ratter. Ain't you, Scully. Hey?"

The little dog slept with him and followed him everywhere. And Miss Sophia and Miss Harriet went out of their way to spoil Willy. He not only knew the streets, he knew the good eateries, and the way to hail a sedan chair if Miss Sophia or Miss Harriet wanted to go out. He knew how much to give the chairmen, where to get a good cup of hot spiced ginger, and, most important, how to guard yourself, when you went about the streets, from footpads—who, I quickly learned, were pickpockets and thieves.

So, then, at least the problem with Willy was solved. I wrote to Uncle Charles and told him so.

But my problem with Mr. Heywood remained.

I had obtained permission to have a grown gentleman caller, but I needed to be alone with him in the parlor.

"Tell 'em 'e's a relative," Willy said.

"I've got so many relatives, Willy. Anyway, his last name is Heywood, and they'll recognize it from the mutiny trials. The names of all those men are known."

"Give 'im a different name. Say 'e's a cousin."

Oh, Willy was not only smart—for anyone could have come up with that—but *daring enough to convince me to do it.*

Still, I went first to Miss Harriet and asked her if she could be the one to greet Captain Heywood when he came. And if she would leave me alone with him in the parlor.

"Yes," she said. "I know who he is."

"I know that you know," I told her. "Because your eyebrows meet. And that means you have second sight. Like my friend Gwen at home."

"Well then, if you keep my secret, I'll keep yours," she said.

Captain Peter Heywood came to call on Friday of the second week I was there. It was a crisp end-of-

September day. The trees were all waiting to be congratulated on their fall dresses. Willy was raking the garden and never even looked up when Captain Heywood came up the walk. But of course Willy had met him already.

And soon enough I found myself in the front parlor, curtsying to a man who had been all of seventeen at the time of the mutiny. And who had been seized on Tahiti along with others and brought back on a horrendous voyage, court-martialed, and then acquitted.

"Mary." He stood up. His eyes passed over me, and I wondered what he was thinking. Perhaps *She looks more like her father than her mother, though there is a bit of the mother there, too.*

"By heaven, you are beautiful," he said. He reached for my hand, kissed it, and sat back down. "Your father would be very proud."

"Captain Heywood," I whispered, "why have you come?"

"I heard from Willy that you were here. I'm setting sail on the HMS *Undaunted* in a few days. Sailing out of Spithead to the West Indies. Four to six weeks each way, depending on the weather. So I had to come. Here, I've brought you a little something."

I opened the wrapping to find a gift. Two books.

One was *The Adventures of Peregrine Pickle.* The other was a Bible.

"Oh, sir, thank you. I didn't have my own Bible, and Miss Harriet and Miss Sophia read from it every night."

But his face was solemn. "It's not just any Bible," he said. "Look at it, please."

I did so. True, it was worn. I thought he'd gotten it out of one of London's bookshops. Then I saw the writing on the inside.

HMS Bounty
Property of Fletcher Christian

The room swayed. Tears came to my eyes. I felt myself transported, lifted to some other place where I could know at least a part of my father. My father had really held this Bible! I looked up at Peter Heywood and knew no thanks were needed. He nodded silently.

"Keep it with you. I've had it since the last time I saw your father, on the sands of Tahiti, when he gave me the message to take home to your grandmother."

There was the answer to the familiarity of his name. Grandmother had spoken once or twice of his coming to visit.

"You came to our house?" I asked.

"Yes. Before you were there. Before you were born, likely. After the trial, in which I was acquitted, I went to your grandmother and to your uncle Edward both. I was the one who pushed your uncle Edward to write his book after the trial."

"Message? What message did you give my grandmother?"

"The message he told me to give her. That he wanted her to know he was completely at fault for what happened. But that he could abide it no more on the ship. That he was in hell with Bligh and had to do it. That he was provoked beyond his ability to cope."

"It sounds so serious, sir."

"It was. The night he left Tahiti, your father stood on the shore with me and gave me this message. And absolved me of any fault in the mutiny also. And he gave me that Bible."

"Why didn't you give it to Grandmother?"

"Because I sensed, talking with her, that she was very bitter about what her son had done. And I bided my time, waiting to give it to someone who would appreciate it. I didn't know who. I might have given it to the Curwens if I hadn't met Willy on the docks the other day. He told me you were here."

"How did Willy know you, sir?"

He laughed. "Willy knows everyone on the docks, in the chophouses, in the netherkens."

"The netherkens?"

"Yes, the neighborhoods, hovels where the poor and the thieves and the riffraff dwell."

I nodded, running my hands over the Bible. Oh Father, I thought, I feel you are so near!

Captain Heywood gave me a moment. Callie came in with some tea and scones and smiled at me. When she had left, Captain Heywood sipped his tea, still watching me. "I've something else to tell you," he said.

I reached for my tea and looked up. "Yes, sir?" Why did I feel suddenly as if there were a volcano on the rug between us?

"Your father has come back to England."

I had to put the teacup aside, my hands were trembling so. "Is it true that you saw him?"

"Yes. I called his name. He turned once. I saw his face in the light of the pine torches on the dock. If it wasn't him, it was his double. And he had that gait, that peculiar way of walking that all the Christian brothers affect. It was his back I recognized, too, when he turned and ran."

"Why did he run?"

"My guess is that he didn't want to involve me. He

must have heard I'm a captain in the navy now, and I think he didn't want me to risk my career, though I'd have risked it in a moment to talk with him."

I paused for a moment, running my hands over the Bible in my lap. "Why are you telling me this, sir?"

"Well, for one, I wanted to see you. Your father was my friend. He trusted me. Second, I wanted to give the Bible to someone before I sailed. And third, Mary, because I think you should know he's in London."

"But nobody knows where."

"There are ways of getting information, Mary. Look how I met Willy. He used to run errands for the officers when ships anchored. I think there is some kind of a pattern to this, don't you?"

Miss Harriet came in then, to ask if anything more was needed. To ask if Captain Heywood wanted a bit of brandy or Madeira. He accepted the Madeira. "Lovely uniform, sir," she said. "All the froufrous on it give it a pattern of authority."

He thanked her. She left. My hands were shaking more now. Miss Harriet was telling me to trust this man; I knew it then.

"I just wanted to tell you: When you go out, keep your eyes open, Mary. And if you get any kind of message, follow up on it. Do you mark me?"

"Yes, sir, and I thank you for coming."

We finished the visit with pleasantries. I told Captain Heywood about the Isle of Man, because he'd come from there as a boy. I told him about Grandmother and Uncle Charles.

And then he left. And it was as if a ghost of my father had been here. My father had once worn that uniform, or one very much like it.

I felt dizzy but comforted as I went upstairs to hide my Bible. No one must see it, ever. It took me only a moment to know where to hide it. I slid it under the mattress of my bed. Then I went to get my best bonnet to go on the Queen's Walk with the others.

ELEVEN

After Captain Heywood left, I yearned to tell someone of his visit. And what he'd told me about my father being in London.

Good news is good, I decided, only if you can share it with someone.

I had no one to share it with, so I went about gloomily. And then I had to avoid Lizzy's cat, because it was always running to me. I had to pat it quickly and give it a tidbit so it would go away.

And then one day I thought of Willy. It wouldn't be giving away any family secrets to tell Willy. He'd been the one to overhear Uncle Charles and me talking in the carriage. And he'd known Captain Heywood and his connection to the family all along. So I did tell Willy.

"I'll keep me eye out fer yer pa," Willy promised.

"You don't know what he looks like."

"I got ears, ain't I?"

"Don't approach him, Willy, if you suspect who he is. He ran from his old friend Heywood. He doesn't want to be found."

"I knows all about people what don't want to be found," he said. "London is full of 'em."

I breathed easier. I could trust Willy.

I soon learned the rhythms of the house and the streets outside, the sounds of those selling wares, when they came to the square, what they sold. With permission, we girls were allowed out to purchase things.

I learned that the bell rung in the square at two in the afternoon was for hot gingerbread. That a man came and set up a gaily striped breakfast stall, with warm buns and tea, for men who might want to leave the house even before their maids were up. Sometimes I rose early and walked Scully for Willy because he'd be mucking out the barn. I'd get some buns—one for me, one for Willy, and one for Miss Harriet, who was always ready for a sweet bun.

After a week or so, I noticed something about Miss Harriet. I no longer thought her ugly. She was funny and dear, and she cared about everyone. Always she dropped a kind word or an amusing one. How could I have ever thought her ugly?

I'd drop Willy's sweet, warm bun off at the barn and run back into the house, to the kitchen, where Miss Harriet would be sipping a cup of tea while Callie was starting breakfast, and we'd sit and have tea before anyone else was up. And we'd talk.

"So, have you heard from your grandmother?"

"I had a letter yesterday. All are well at home."

Lessons were not too difficult. I'd already had French and some Latin, knew the poets of the time, and studied history in my school in Douglas. And between that and what I'd learned from Grandmother and Uncle Charles, I was able to keep in stride. I was even doing well in art classes once a week, across the square with Miss Reynolds. I was doing a pencil sketch of Dick Turpin.

And then one morning, just as we were all bored with learning when James Watts invented the steam engine, or studying the marvels of astronomy or Captain Cook's voyage, Miss Harriet spotted a strange black carriage in the square and interrupted the class to take us outside.

"I've heard of this man, girls. He's a newcomer to the list of peddlers. His name is Dr. Katterfelt. I think he is a quack, on the same level as occultists, and nurses and other people trained in medicine outside the universities. But he's an interesting quack. He has theories. Be nice to him."

So we all trooped outside to see the quack with theories.

Dr. Katterfelt drove a black coach pulled by a pair of handsome black horses. He wore a white wig, black breeches, and a rather worn coat, and he sported a beard. Peering out the windows of the coach and sitting on his lap up front were black cats, at least two dozen of them, some of them kittens.

He put on a show for a shilling or two. Miss Harriet told Callie to bring out some bowls of milk for the cats. And we stood in the square, pulling our shawls about us, and watched as the good Dr. Katterfelt put a drop or two of water into a dish and held it under what he called a *microscope*, and showed us the properties of the water. We oohed and aahed while he explained microscopes and told us how doctors all around the world would someday be using them.

He had other toys, too, that he displayed on a table he set up then and there. A small telescope, a celestial globe, and an orrery. "This is named for Charles Boyle," he said, holding up the orrery. "The Earl of Orrery, he was, who owned one of the fanciest models of the solar system. And it *moved*, to illustrate eclipses and planetary orbits."

He was well-spoken. We girls conjectured afterward that *he* was the Earl of Orrery, thrown out of his manor house by his wife, reduced to being a peddler because of gambling debts, and looking for a benefactress. Who would it be? Which of us?

I discovered that Celeste had a fanciful imagination. She said he had come to see Miss Harriet, who was so beautiful inside that he didn't need a microscope to see her soul.

Fanny said he'd come because he knew she was the daughter of Maria Edgeworth and wanted to meet her. Sibella said no, he wanted to meet her mother, Lady Hamilton. Alice said he had come to see her, that he had a friend in Newgate about to be hanged and he wanted to meet her father.

Lizzy said it was her father, Charles Lamb, he wanted to meet.

"What about you, Mary?" they asked me.

"He wants to meet my uncle Edward," I joked.

We all laughed.

"It's my father," Jane said. "He wants to be an actor and has found out my father performs at Covent Garden Theatre."

We laughed so much.

Dr. Katterfelt came every Wednesday. He taught us that there are two types of nebulae. One is made up of a cloud of gas lit by a single star, and the other is made of groups of stars that appear to be large white masses of light if the telescope is not superior.

He brought us pamphlets and told us about William Herschel and his sister Caroline, who located eight hundred and forty-eight double stars. About the half-ton telescope that William Herschel used to find a new ring around Saturn.

Every week we went out to greet him. And I never looked at the stars carelessly again.

And then, one day, Langston sent a note around. It was written on creamy vellum. "Would you accompany me to the theater?" it read.

Miss Harriet and Miss Sophia had a rule. A student could not leave the school with a male unless he was a close relative, or unless a chaperone accompanied them.

It was decided that Jane was to be the chaperone, since we would see her father perform.

So permission was given.

Lizzy was insanely jealous. She had wanted to be picked to go with me. "I suppose you think you're Miss Fancy-Boots, going to the theater with a young man from Cambridge," Lizzy said, approaching me in the hall after I'd dressed.

"No, I've never been Miss Fancy-Boots."

"There is something about you," she said, eyeing me warily. "I don't know what, but I'll find out. You're trouble, is what. You carry scandal like a lady carries her reticule. And you'll bring disgrace to this school yet."

I sighed. "Lizzy, I wouldn't know how. I'm just a country girl from the Isle of Man."

"Well, you are that! I'll allow it. But that doesn't mean you still can't bring scandal. And I'll be the first one to sniff it out."

"Lizzy, why do you lay siege to me so?"

"Because until you came, I was the one who had the air of mystery, with my father being Charles Lamb. Now it's all you. They don't even care about me anymore."

"Lizzy, everyone cares for you."

"Posh." And she swished by me. "You're hiding something, Mary Christian. And I'll find out what it is and unmask you. I promise."

I was never so glad to see Langston. I ran to him to hug him, then stopped myself. That would never do. So I allowed him to kiss my hand as a proper young student at Cambridge would do, then introduced him to Miss Harriet and Miss Sophia. "We plundered birds' nests together, growing up," I told them. "We gathered hazelnuts and read about Robin Hood."

"Wonderful," Miss Harriet said.

We went to an early performance of *Hamlet*, played by Jane's father, John Philip Kemble, at the Covent Garden Theatre. Then Jane got us backstage to meet the great man, and I thrilled when he put his arms around her and kissed her. Oh, to have a father!

It was when we were in a tearoom that Langston gave me the letter.

"The Curwens mailed me this to give to you," he said.

It was in a deplorable state, stained and wrinkled. And the writing was like that of a schoolboy.

It was from my brother, Thursday October!

"Dere Mary," it said,

I have learn to write from Mr. Adams, who teaches all the children. I have wed two years past now. Her name is Susannah. She was first the wife of Young, then of Quintal. You are too young to kno them. I have my own child, a girl I name Mary. Our mother is still good. I hope you are happy to get this leter. McCoy throw himself off the cliffs near our fathers old house. Quintal said he would kill me and brother Charles unless he could have our mother for his woman. He was killed by Young to make peace, which we have now. A British ship came by and the Captain give me letter from our father. Give me address to write to you. Say my letter go through many people but will get to you.

Your brother,
Thursday October Christian

I folded the letter and put it in my reticule. I could not let Langston or Jane see it. It was barbaric, no less. Why would Thursday October write to me? I scarcely remembered him. Did he expect me to write back?

But he was my brother.

136

Only if I wanted him to be, I decided. And I hadn't broken the tie. It had been broken for me. My father had put his life in danger, bringing me to England to get me away from my family.

I looked around the tearoom, with its ruffled calico curtains, its multipaned windows, its shelves lined with books, the round-faced lady who ran it behind a counter piled high with iced cakes. I thought of the play I had just seen. And I thought, *Father, wherever you are, thank you for bringing me here. Oh, thank you!*

And I smiled at Langston and Jane, held up my chin, and spoke of other matters. Then we went into the street, and I managed to keep on a good face so they would suspect nothing. And Langston hailed a coach to take us home.

All went well until Langston took us to the door and said good-night.

He hugged me warmly, there in the shadows. I smelled the pipe smoke on his jacket and hugged him back. "Oh, Langston," I said, "I want to go back to Man and stand on the quay and watch the fishing fleet come in."

"I'd be on it," he said.

"Would you want to be there, too?"

"In a way. But I also want to move forward with my life. And you must, too, Mary."

He kissed my forehead, promised to call again, and went down the steps.

As Callie opened the door to let Jane and me in, Miss Harriet was there to greet us. "Whatever it was he gave you, hide it well," she whispered.

I was not surprised. And I did hide the letter well. That very night. I hid it in a tin of tea that Uncle Charles had given me, a cunning tin canister. I hid the letter under the tea leaves, then put the tin under my bed. Now I had two items to guard, and I'd guard them with my life.

⌁ TWELVE

Once a week either Miss Harriet or Miss Sophia took us on an outing. To Bloomsbury, where the artists and intellectuals met. We'd go to tea, and then watch an artist working in the fresh air. Or we'd go to Bloomsbury's Montagu House, otherwise known as The British Museum. To Soho Square. To Carlisle House, where Theresa Cornelys held her masquerades, and Sir Joseph Banks had his museum. Or just plain shopping. Sometimes we walked to the splendid tradesmen's shops not far from St. James's Square and spent our money on scarves, new hats, books, or other furbelows.

One lovely day in mid-October, Lizzy pleaded sick

and desired to stay home from a shopping trip. It was not like Lizzy. She loved shopping.

We had a lovely day, but when I came home, I found that my letter from Thursday October was missing.

It was not in the canister of tea.

The reason I looked for the letter was because my room was disheveled, as if it had been searched. Obviously it had been.

Lizzy had my letter from Thursday October. She knew who I was!

I had to sit down and think. My head was spinning. I had to confront her quietly, so the whole school wouldn't know. The girls were downstairs having supper after our return from shopping. I'd been sent up to see how Lizzy was faring.

I knocked on the door of her room.

"Enter."

She was lying on her bed with Dick Turpin. Smiling at me.

"How are you, Lizzy?"

"Middling well."

I stepped into the room and closed the door behind me. "I'll come right to it without alerting the rest of the house. My room's been searched. A letter is missing."

Her smile got craftier. "You mean a letter from Pitcairn Island? From your brother Thursday October?"

And she reached under her pillow and drew it out.

I stepped forward. "Give it to me. It's mine. You had no right."

"Oh, and what are you going to do? Tell our teachers? And have Miss Sophia or Miss Harriet read it? And she read parts of it: "'Dere Mary, I have learn to write. . . . I have wed two years past now. . . . McCoy throw himself off the cliffs near our fathers old house.'"

She waved the letter in front of her. "I knew you were carrying scandal about with you. I smelled it. So your father is Fletcher Christian, then."

"Lizzy, give me the letter, please."

"I could get you thrown out of here for hiding your true identity."

"Nobody would believe you. All the girls make up identities."

"But yours is notorious. Your father is wanted by the King. And if that is found out, the scandal could get the school closed. You know that, don't you?"

"Why would you want to do that? You live here. It's your home."

"We'd live in Drury Lane Theater. Or next to it.

Miss Sophia's blank-verse tragedy is opening there in the new season."

"You're bluffing."

Lizzy boosted herself up on one elbow. "I have an obligation to tell them who you are. If someone discovers it, the scandal could ruin them! Unless, of course . . ."

I felt weak. "Unless what?"

"Unless you convince them to let me go on my holiday with my father."

I stared at her. "You really *are* the daughter of Charles Lamb?"

"I don't lie as you do. But then, I've nothing to be ashamed of."

I ran my tongue over my lips, which were dry now. "You mean if I convince them to allow you to go on your holiday, you won't tell?"

"Yes. But I won't give back the letter, either."

"Why? What do you want with it?"

Lizzy got off the bed. She stood in front of her mirror and brushed her hair. Then she unbuttoned the front of her dress and put the letter inside her chemise. "I'm nobody's fool, Mary Christian. This is where you should have kept your letter. The trouble with you is that you don't know anything about intrigue. You're an innocent. Why won't I give it back? Think. Call it insurance."

I didn't have to think. "You mean you're going to use it to make me do your bidding."

She sighed. "Whatever do you mean? Just say I'm keeping it safe so the school won't be closed. That's insurance, isn't it? Now, come, let's go down to supper. I'm starved."

I knew when I was bested. To make matters worse, every time Lizzy looked at me, she smiled. Her victory was mortally sweet.

That very night, I sought out Miss Sophia and Miss Harriet before going to bed to ask if Lizzy could have her holiday. After evening prayers, our time was private. I knew that Miss Sophia and Miss Harriet were in their private quarters, writing. And they were to be bothered only in extreme emergencies.

I had contrived what I was to say to them. And I was ready as I knocked on the door and was told to enter.

Miss Sophia and Miss Harriet looked up from their desks. "Yes, Mary, what is it?"

So I told them. I wasn't about to scruple or hesitate a moment in order to keep my family secret. Lie? I knew how to do it. So I told them all about how Lizzy's ailment today was because her father had written and asked her to come. He *did* have need of her. She had showed me the letter.

I knew, you see, that these two good women had a rule that all letters from home were to be considered sacred and private. And there was to be no intrusion on that privacy.

"Her father is Charles Lamb," I concluded.

"We know, child," Miss Harriet said.

They said they would study the matter. They said they were glad to see me taking Lizzy's side. That it was encouraging. And so I left with some hope, anyway.

But Miss Harriet looked at me in a funny way. I'd have to be careful now with her, I decided. She was too smart. I'd have to keep lying to her, and I didn't like it.

And so Lizzy got her holiday.

"Where is the letter?" I asked Lizzy when I went to her room, supposedly to help her pack. "You're not taking it with you."

"It's hidden here in my room," she said. "I can't take it with me. If my father found it, he'd not be happy with me. And I do wish to make him happy with me. Isn't that how you feel about your father?"

"I haven't seen him since I was five," I said. "And I don't expect to see him ever again."

She smirked at me. "I'll be gone only two days. I heard Miss Harriet say that when I come back, we're having a class on Coleridge's *Ancient Mariner*. That ought to be something."

"Lizzy, if you dare!"

She tossed her hair. "Oh, I'll think of something else for you to do for me so I daren't," she promised.

Lizzy was gone for two days, and when her carriage rounded the fountain in the middle of the square and drew up in front of the house, we stood with our noses pressed against the window to see if she would bring in her father, Charles Lamb.

"Girls, girls, it isn't proper!" Miss Harriet scolded. So we drew back.

But nobody came inside the door with Lizzy but Enfield.

"Why didn't you bring in Charles Lamb?" the girls chorused.

"Oh, he's much too busy," she said. "He took me today to the Tower to see the royal animals. I saw tigers and lions and elephants."

All the girls listened. "And," she went on, looking

past them to me, "he told me he went to school with Coleridge. To Christ's Hospital School. And my father's family was nearby and sent in all kinds of small comforts, which he shared with Coleridge because Coleridge's family was far away and he had none."

We ran to the windows as the coach pulled away. A man's face peered out from the carriage window. A slender white hand pushed the velvet curtain aside. Then the curtain closed. I shivered.

"It's him, all right." It was Miss Harriet, looking over my shoulder.

I felt a new sense of regard for Lizzy.

"Good, you can tell us about your father tomorrow in class," Miss Harriet said.

"But we're supposed to study Coleridge!" This from Jane.

"I'd rather not make my father a subject for class, if it pleases you," said Lizzy. And she made a dramatic exit.

The next day in literature class we spoke of Samuel Taylor Coleridge, the man who had written *The Rime of the Ancient Mariner*, the poem that some people said was written about *my* father. Miss Harriet had taken me aside and gotten my permission first. "We don't want to embarrass you by speaking of your uncle," she said.

I looked at the floor. I told her it would not embarrass

me. I told her the girls were so looking forward to it.

"Is there something you want to tell me, Mary?" she asked softly. "You can, you know."

I did look at her then, at the face I'd first thought ugly but that no longer appeared that way to me now. Oh, how I wished I could tell her!

"You've some kind of burden." It was not a question. I nodded my head yes.

"I can't get a purchase on what it is. But you know you can come to me anytime, don't you?"

I said yes, and that seemed to satisfy her. Then I sought out Lizzy and told her that if she dared give me away, I would pull her hair out, scandal or no scandal.

"Of course I won't," she promised. "But I'm thinking of another favor you can do for me. Oh, I know! Ask Miss Harriet if we can invite Coleridge to the school! And when he comes, you must tell him I'm the daughter of Charles Lamb. And I just know he'll do something special for me!"

> *I moved, and could not feel my limbs:*
> *I was so light—almost*
> *I thought that I had died in sleep,*
> *And was a blessed ghost.*

Was the poem written about my father? Was this the way my father had felt on the *Bounty*? I know he had met Coleridge. Grandmother had told me. Had they conferred, then, and had Coleridge listened to his story?

> *Oh! dream of joy! is this indeed*
> *The light-house top I see?*
> *Is this the hill? is this the kirk?*
> *Is this mine own countree!*

Was this my father, on coming home?

I was under a spell. We were all spellbound, hearing of clear-as-glass harbors and moonlight steeped in silence.

> *He prayeth best, who loveth best,*
> *All things both great and small;*
> *For the dear God who loveth us*
> *He made and loveth all.*

Some girls were dabbing away tears by now. But Miss Harriet went on to finish the poem, then closed the book. "Well, and so now we must learn all we can learn about Mr. Coleridge."

"Is it really about Mary's uncle?" asked Jane.

"We don't know," said Miss Harriet. "Only Mr. Coleridge knows."

They were all looking at me in envy. Lizzie was looking, too—in malice.

"Why don't I write and ask Mr. Coleridge to come to visit our school?" I put forth weakly.

"Oh," said Jane, "we can all write."

It was decided quickly and enthusiastically. We would all write individual letters to Mr. Coleridge, asking him to come. He need write back only one letter to us all.

Within a week he wrote. One letter.

To me.

"You should be honored," Miss Harriet said.

"You must greet him at the door and personally serve his tea," said Miss Sophia.

"I hate you. What did you put in that letter?" said Lizzy.

"I think it's great sport." This from Jane.

"So do I," added Fanny.

"Can we wear something special instead of these blue dresses?" asked Sibella.

"We should wear our blue dresses. My father said

that at Christ's Hospital School, the boys wore long blue mantles and were called blue-coat boys." Thus spake Lizzy, and all agreed. So we wore our blue dresses for Mr. Coleridge when he came two weeks later.

It was November. The skies over London were gray and threatening. And I thought of Coleridge's poetry, from which I'd memorized some lines:

> *The thin grey cloud is spread on high,*
> *It covers but not hides the sky.*

Someone banged the brass door knocker. I opened the door. And there stood Mr. Coleridge.

He was smaller than I'd imagined. He took off his hat to reveal curly brown hair. He wore a wide cravat, silk and pure white, tied in a bow. And a black great-coat. He carried a fancy cane.

"Welcome, Mr. Coleridge. Welcome to our school. I am Mary Christian, niece of Mr. Fletcher Christian."

He bowed and came in. The girls parted as the waters had parted for Moses. Miss Harriet took his greatcoat and handed it to Callie. "It's warmest in the front parlor," she said. "And we have high tea."

He told us everything.

We sat on the floor around his feet in our blue

dresses. I did not spill the tea when I served it, and was ready with his second cup when he was ready for it. He used snuff, and his cane had a gold handle. Grandmother would have said he was the perfect example of English decadence. But what he told us with that first cup of tea!

"I had nine siblings. My father was a vicar, and my older brother Frank had a love of beating me up. I was a mopey, dreamy, and lonely child. Once I had a putrid fever. I saw four angels around my bed. Another time I had a fight with Frank because he ruined my slice of cheese. I ran to attack him with a knife and my mother grabbed me by the arm, but I got away and went sulking. I went to a hill below which the Otter flows, about a mile from home. I said my prayers and gloated because everyone must be miserable. I fell asleep and rolled to within three yards of the river. More tea, please."

I jumped to my feet and served it. He smiled up at me. "So you are the girl I wrote to?"

"Yes, sir."

"Well, we must speak later."

With the second cup of tea he told us more.

"So the crier from the town of Ottery cried out that I was missing. People from two nearby villages joined the

Ottery people in the search, which went on all night. They found me, next morning, nearly frozen. I couldn't walk. And I've suffered from the ague ever since."

"Did you like Christ's Hospital School?" Fanny asked.

"Oh, dear me, no. My father died, so I had to go there. I was but ten. If not for my older brother George, who looked after me like a father, I'd have died. I remember"—he set down his teacup and leaned forward—"how terrible whole-day leaves were."

"Whole-day leaves?" asked Jane.

"Yes. They'd turn us out for the whole day on holidays. Most of the boys had homes to go to. I didn't. So I and others like me wandered London's streets. Summer holidays we'd swim in the river, but during winter holidays we were lost and hungry and cold. Then there were the floggings."

"Floggings?" I asked.

"Yes. The Reverend Boyer, the headmaster, was fond of flogging. He'd go at us for the least provocation. Oh, yes."

"And you wore blue mantles, like our dresses," Sibella put in.

He smiled. "Well, not like your dresses, but blue, yes."

Then Lizzy nudged me, so I had to tell him. "Lizzy's father is Charles Lamb. He went to school with you."

"Ah yes, Charles. He was one of the lucky boys with family nearby. How is he?"

"Well, sir," Lizzy said.

Then he spoke of his poetry.

I could not ask if he knew my "Uncle Fletcher," for that might imply that my father was in England. But he told us how he was intimate with William Wordsworth and his sister, Dorothy, and how Wordsworth knew the Christians.

It was enough. He looked at me and recited:

"Water, water, every where,
And all the boards did shrink;
Water, water, every where,
Nor any drop to drink."

While he recited this, he looked at me steadfastly. His eyes locked with mine. And in that moment I realized that he knew. He knew I was Fletcher Christian's daughter!

I remembered that Grandmother had once said my father had met with Wordsworth when he came back to England.

I flushed and smiled, then properly lowered my gaze.

Lizzy, of course, saw the look between us. She nudged me again.

"Sir," I was forced to say, "Lizzy would like something signed from you."

"Can't Lizzy speak for herself?" he asked.

Now Lizzy flushed. "I'm shy, sir."

The other girls all hissed, and Mr. Coleridge smiled. "I shall sign something for each of you," he said. Quickly the girls got up and ran to get something to be signed. I rose slowly. He reached out his hand. I looked at Miss Harriet, who nodded permission, and I gave him my hand. He took it gently and held it.

"Keep your secrets well," he said. "As I have kept mine. Sometimes they are a comfort; sometimes they are an albatross around our necks."

"Yes, sir," I said.

Miss Harriet nodded in agreement.

Then he took a copy of *Lyrical Ballads*, in which *The Ancient Mariner* was published, and signed it for me.

Now I had another treasure. I would put it under my mattress, I decided, with the *Bounty* Bible, and keep it from Lizzy's sight.

But when the girls came back, Lizzy quickly spied

the book in my hands. Later, she accosted me in the hall.

"He signed a book for you!"

"He wrote a famous poem about my uncle."

"My father gave him small comforts when he was a starving boy at Christ's Hospital School! Let me see the book!" she demanded.

There was nothing for it but to comply. "Keep your secrets well," he had written.

"Not if I have anything to say about it!" Lizzy taunted me.

I did something I should not have done then. I slapped her in the face. Oh, she set up a howling, and quickly the Misses Harriet and Sophia responded.

In lieu, and perhaps in fear, of summoning Uncle Edward again, Miss Sophia put me in my room and said I must stay there for two days. I was to be let out only to go to the necessary.

THIRTEEN

Two days in my room! It was worse than Newgate Prison! At first I cried. Then I remembered that I must write to Gwen. She had written, and I hadn't replied. So I did that. Then I wrote to Uncle Charles, telling him that Willy and Scully were doing fine. To John Curwen, telling him about our rat boy, whose condition had been more dolorous than the chimney sweeps he was so worried about. Then to Grandmother. And then I slept and dreamed I was home, running with Langston to a nearby stream, where we would spend the day fishing.

When I awoke, I heard a commotion in the square and looked out my window, expecting to see Dr.

Katterfelt. Today was Wednesday. Had he come when I slept? But it was only the orange girl. Oh, how I longed for an orange!

I examined my treasures and even read a bit of my father's Bible. One page was turned down and tattered. A verse from Second Samuel where the word "exile" was marked. Is that the way my father felt? As if he were in exile?

I cried again. Then I decided to be Mary, Queen of Scots, for a while. I pretended I was in the house of William Fletcher, Grandmother's ancestor; that I'd just fled my kingdom; and that I'd just been given red velvet to make a gown for my beheading.

Then I became bored and decided to be Mary Wollstonecraft, writing her book *Thoughts on the Education of Daughters*. Maybe I would write a book someday. I'd write that daughters should never be punished.

I read the London *Times* that had been left outside my door. We were supposed to read it every day. And every day I looked at the small items, hoping for news of my father. On the second day I sighted something else.

The Cat Man was in the hospital, it said! Dr. Katterfelt!

It seems he had fallen from his carriage when it had collided with another one, and now he was found to be weak and unable to walk. He was in Guy's Hospital. Oh, I hoped he wasn't hurt badly! And what had happened to his cats? I must go and see him.

So I devised a plan. Miss Sophia had spoken to us of doing charity work. I would suggest a project in which we visited the sick. And I would go to Guy's.

I think I would have gone mad another hour in the room if Miss Harriet hadn't knocked on my door shortly afterward.

"So, how does it feel to be a prisoner?"

"Terrible."

"Have you repented of your sins?" As always, her voice was filled with amusement.

"Miss Harriet, I have the most wonderful idea for a charity project," I told her.

"Have you, now? I told my sister one day would be enough to turn you around. Tell me about it."

A meeting was held in Morals and Philosophy class the next day. The girls received my idea with enthusiasm, and Miss Sophia said that if this was what a day's confinement in one's room brought about, perhaps all the girls should have one.

I didn't tell them about Dr. Katterfelt.

Everyone immediately decided which hospital

they would visit. I, of course, had Guy's, because I had the perfect guide and male to accompany me.

Willy.

Everyone had to be accompanied by an adult. It was times like these that Miss Harriet and Miss Sophia called upon the rich ladies in the square who liked to donate their time to the school. At first they were both against my being escorted by Willy, until I pointed out how he knew his way around better than any adult. "Guy's Hospital is in southeast London," I concluded. "And Willy is the only one among us who knows his way around there."

"Very well," Miss Sophia said.

"What are you up to?" Miss Harriet asked, taking me aside. "I, too, saw the paper and the article about Dr. Katterfelt. Is it him you're seeking?"

She was too smart by half for me. I admitted it was, and she promised not to tell, and I loved her even more for it.

"But you all must have partners," she said to the class. "And I would like you to take Lizzy as your partner, Mary."

I groaned inwardly, but I couldn't complain. I was having my own way in everything else, wasn't I? I was so elated, I felt like an exile being welcomed home.

※　　※　　※

"One day in yer room? I'm surprised they didn't flog ye," Willy said when I went to find him in the carriage house later that day.

"They don't flog. Willy, I've something to tell you." And so I told him about Dr. Katterfelt, swearing him to secrecy. Then I told him Miss Harriet and Miss Sophia were going to ask him to accompany me and Lizzy to Guy's Hospital.

"A fine place for a genteel girl the likes o' you," he said. "The patients there capture lice and pit them against each other in races."

"Willy, I don't care. Dr. Katterfelt is there."

"And why do ye care so much about 'im?"

Why, indeed? I had yet to ask myself why a cry of dismay had gone through me at learning of his fate. And why I knew I must go and visit him.

He scowled at me. "Not to worry, lass. I'll go with ye." And then Miss Harriet summoned him inside.

Miss Sophia insisted we wear our white caps and aprons, and old-fashioned neckerchiefs under our warm cloaks and winter hats. She gave us handkerchiefs soaked in vinegar to hold over our faces. "Don't touch anything," she warned us. "I have written ahead saying you are coming, and the place you are going to has been well cleaned."

Willy nudged me in the ribs.

"Stay only an hour." Miss Sophia handed a basket of food to Willy, a basket of clean men's clothing to Lizzy, and a basket of remedies to me. "Now, I've told you, Mary and Lizzy, in that basket are Goddard's Drops, Dr. Anderson's True Scots Pills, Daffy's Elixir, and Dr. Bateman's Drops. Give them all to the patient you are assigned to."

Willy looked almost like the young scion of a wealthy family, dressed as he was in the new breeches and frock coat the Misses Sophia and Harriet had gotten for him. He even wore a jaunty cap, and on his back, soldier-style, was strapped a rolled-up blanket. I figured it was for Lizzy's and my laps if the weather turned colder.

Willy directed the driver to southeast London with an air of experience. Along the way, he pointed out things to us—timber yards, breweries, dyeworks. He knew all the alleys: Hairbrain Court, Money Bag Alley, Hog Yard.

As we drew up in front of Guy's Hospital, he had a paper to show the guards at the iron gates. Inside, there was another guardhouse and another paper to show. We dismissed our coach, and Willy told the guard that for an extra shilling, he should have another coach waiting for us in an hour. The man was glad to comply.

A fat man, who introduced himself simply as Shillingworth, took us into the main entrance, where there were more questions, but Willy answered them with aplomb and we were shown down a large, dark, cavernous hallway. The place suddenly took on the look of a castle, complete with pine-knot torches on the high walls.

I saw Willy take Mr. Shillingworth aside at one point and tip him too, and it worked, because after we had passed room after iron-gated room, Mr. Shillingworth stopped, took out his large ring of keys, and unlocked one gate, leaving it open.

"Here's a man what needs help and visitors," he said. "His name is Katterfelt."

"Ohhh!" Lizzy cried. But I nudged her well and she hushed.

"Dr. Katterfelt?" I asked cautiously. I went slowly inside, dragging Lizzy with me. "What's happened to you?"

His bed was a mattress covered with ticking. He had one thin blanket. Then I knew what the blanket on Willy's back was for. I watched him unstrap it and hand it to Dr. Katterfelt.

"'Ere you are, mate," he said. "From the Misses Hartsdale."

Slowly and painfully, the man sat up, took the blanket, fingered it as if he'd never seen such a thing before, and then looked at us. It was the first I'd ever seen his hair. It was mussed, of course. It was brown, not white as I'd supposed it to be under that wig he'd always worn.

And it made his face look younger. He reminded me of someone, as a matter of fact. But who?

Lizzy stepped forward and handed him her basket of clothing. "For you, sir."

He took it and thanked her.

We stepped back. He stood, with some difficulty. Willy helped him to a nearby chair, and gave him some of the food that had been sent. He ate some bread and cheese and ham, and drank from a flask that I'd seen Miss Harriet sneak into the basket.

"How can I thank you?"

"We miss you," I said.

He looked at us all thoroughly then. "Oh!" he said, brightening. "You're the children from the school on the square."

"That's right." Lizzy giggled. I'd never heard her giggle before.

"And you." He pointed a slender finger at me. "You are one of them."

"Yes," I answered. But the way he'd said *them* put me on notice. What did he mean? Never mind; he was feverish. I gave him the medicines, and he looked through them and took some of one of the medicines. He seemed to know what they were. "My brother is a doctor," he said.

A jolt went through me; then I shook it away.

"These are good, children." He smiled and shook a finger at Willy. "I know you, sir. You've come a way in the world, it seems."

Willy smiled. "They're good to me."

"And Old Nettlemouth hasn't found you, then?"

"No," Willy said. "Not so far, he ain't."

I handed Dr. Katterfelt a small Bible that I'd found under the medicines in my basket. "For you, sir."

He took it, opened it, and flipped through it as we waited.

And then he found the page he wanted. "Ah, here it

is—Second Samuel," he said. "'Thou art a stranger, and also an exile.'" Before he was finished, his voice was coming as if from very far away, way above me, getting fainter and fainter, while my legs got weaker and weaker and a cold sweat broke out on my forehead.

It was then that my knees buckled and I fell to the floor.

When I looked up, my father was peering down at me.

∽ FOURTEEN

I knew it the way I knew the sun would come up in the morning. The way you know you will get a stomachache if you eat too many strawberries with sugar on them.

The way you know it when somebody's eyes find yours and you are locked forever with them in this life. And maybe even the next one.

Everyone was leaning over me. Lizzy was crying. "Oh, she hit her head! Oh, somebody do something!" *Lizzy was crying for me!*

Well, she always was a Miss Sissy-Boots anyway. I started to get up, but everything in the dolorous little room was spinning. Next thing I knew, a matron came,

166

in an apron and cap that were whiter than an angel's, but with anything but an angel's voice. "Out of the way, everybody!"

She looked like Satan's nursemaid, if he had one. And everyone got out of the way while she lifted me off the cold floor, held one hand behind my back, and put something under my nose to bring me to life again. The back of my head hurt.

"I'm all right," I said.

She thrust a fat, stubby hand in front of my face. "Can you see?"

"Yes."

"Can you hear?"

"You should have asked that one first."

"Don't be a sassy little thing or I'll not allow you to visit again. You're not fit to be in this place. It often affects females that way."

"I'm not a fainting female," I said. And I stood up.

She turned to Willy and Lizzy. "I'd advise you to get your friend out of here now." And with that she turned and took her leave, and the four of us remained, staring at one another in embarrassment.

"What happened?" Lizzy asked.

"I don't know." I knew I must watch myself with her. She mustn't know Dr. Katterfelt was my father.

My father was staring at me.

"If you all will leave me with Dr. Katterfelt for a moment," I begged, "I want to ask him something."

Lizzy hesitated, but Willy pulled her out of the little room. They went out into the hall, and I turned my attention to the thin man sitting on the edge of his bed. "How are your cats?" I asked, for lack of anything else to say.

"They are well, thank you. They are cared for here. The hospital is in need of good mousers here, and so the good turn is justified."

He spoke carefully. I noticed that his face had the same cast as that of Uncle Charles. That the voice, now when he wasn't acting, had the same timbre. "It's why you limp, isn't it?" I asked him.

"What's that?"

"So I won't see the gait you have that Uncle Charles has, and Uncle Edward. All the Christian men have it."

"Miss, I don't know what you're talking about, I assure you."

"You're not Dr. Katterfelt. You're my father, Fletcher Christian," I whispered.

"Fletcher Christian!" He made an impatient gesture

with his hand. "I've heard of him. Look, miss, they may be able to hang all kinds of charges on me, but not that. He's a wanted man."

The way he said it, *wanted man*, warned me. "All right," I answered, "but you are my father."

"Child, I'm sorry you don't know where your father is. But I am not he."

"I know you've been back in England. Everyone knows it. I have your Bible. That's how I know who you are. Captain Heywood came around to the school and gave it to me, and I found the page, so used and marked. And the verse you read just now from Second Samuel. That's how I know who you are."

"Dear child, don't upset yourself so. I don't know about any Captain Heywood or marked Bible. I am grateful for your visit, but perhaps it was too much for you and you oughtn't to come again."

"I came to see Dr. Katterfelt. I came to do a charitable project for the school. I picked this place because I knew Dr. Katterfelt was here. I read it in the papers."

"The papers?" He was dismayed.

"Yes, they had an article on Dr. Katterfelt's being hurt and in here. You're known about town, you and your cats. But I know now why you came to the school. To see me, isn't that why? Your very own daughter?"

He stood up. "Child, you should go. And continue your project elsewhere."

"Don't put me off, please. Let me come to see you. I won't tell anyone anything."

He looked at me, unsure. I could see he wanted me to come back as much as I wanted to come. "Dr. Katterfelt," I added.

He smiled. And I saw Uncle Charles in the smile and in the eyes now. Oh, how it warmed me. "Anything," I said, "I'll call you anything if you let me come back. I'll call you George the Third, if you require it."

He smiled. "That won't be necessary. You are a feisty little thing, aren't you?"

"I've had to be."

He nodded, lowering his eyes.

"How are your cats, truly?" I asked again.

"My cats are fine."

"And how long do you expect to be here, Dr. Katterfelt?"

"Until my leg heals and I gain back my strength."

"Do you need anything?"

"No."

"I shall bring more medicines."

"Yes, do. Thank you, child, thank you."

I felt his hand on my shoulder as I walked out.

On the way home, Willy and Lizzy spoke for a while in the carriage, but it was halfhearted talk. Then we all fell silent and dozed.

I woke first. There seemed to be some commotion on London's streets as we came to the mercantile section near Fleet Street and the Strand. Our carriage was held up in traffic. Carriages were jammed all over the streets, with drivers yelling, horses whinnying, and street boys running about among them, trying to help out and earn a shilling. Our driver got down from his seat to see what was happening, and Willy got out to hold the horses' reins.

Back inside, Willy told us the news that would turn our world upside down for the next two weeks and allow me to escape the school and go to visit Dr. Katterfelt several more times: "Covent Garden Theatre is on fire!"

"Oh, no!" Lizzy sat forward, trying to see something, but only traffic and crowds were to be seen from the window. "Miss Sophia knows all those people."

"Never mind Miss Sophia," I said. "What about Jane's father?"

"They're saying twenty-two people were killed," Willy told us.

We looked in the direction of the theater. Sparks and smoke were rising to the sky. Ladder companies were on their way, with horses pulling wagons that were filled with buckets. A crowd was already assembling on the streets leading to it. Women were opening upstairs windows and peering out. The City Watch and the magistrates were trying to hold people back, and then along came the King's Guard to help.

"A fine opportunity to do a little pickpocketing," Willy said wistfully, "but we'd best get you two home first."

I didn't know if he was serious or teasing. It took what seemed hours for us to get home, what with the crowds and the halting of traffic. And when we got there, Miss Sophia was gone. Miss Harriet was in charge, and there was an air of excitement in the house.

"Miss Sophia has gone to her friends' aid," Miss Harriet told us. "She may be bringing some of them home this night. She left orders for you and Lizzy to double up in your rooms, Mary. Come on, we're setting up more beds and cots."

"How is Jane?" I asked.

"Miss Sophia took her to find her father."

Lessons were put on hold, and once again I found myself in a room with Lizzy. We were exhausted from moving beds and making them up, from helping Callie and Dorothy, the kitchen maid, to prepare cakes and tea and sandwiches for any stragglers Miss Sophia might bring home. Lizzy looked at me just before we blew out the candles that night.

"I know who he is," she said.

"Who?"

"The man we met today in the hospital."

"Yes. He's Dr. Katterfelt."

"No," she said. "He's your father, Fletcher Christian. I heard you talking to him."

I gasped. "Where was Willy?"

"Gone to fetch a chaise. Now you are completely under my sway. And I want a favor."

⌒ FIFTEEN

Covent Garden Theatre was a place beloved by all of London. Even I knew that seats in the boxes went for five shillings, seats in the pit for three, and a gallery ticket could be had for two, or even one in the upper gallery. That the theater wasn't just for the genteel, but for the masses as well.

The next morning, our school was organized chaos. Jane was back, and we were so glad to see her that we crowded around her, still in our nightgowns, in the upstairs hall.

"My father is alive, but devastated," she told us. "Fifteen of his workers were killed. The rest of the

174

twenty-two were fighting the fire. He's downstairs now. Oh, I must dress. I'm sorry. So many of my family are downstairs. Miss Sophia has taken them in. Part of our home was destroyed, too."

She acted as if all the chaos in our school were her fault. And it was chaos. Breakfast was catch-as-catch-can. We sat down at the table in the formal dining room with people in long capes and lavish clothing that smelled of smoke.

"They're all Kembles," Celeste whispered. She was excited. She had grown up on tragedy and greeted it like an old friend. "Let's take our dishes and leave these poor people to their sorrow," she said. So we did. We sat on the stairway and on the floor, and stared. One woman had a baby. She wore a long silk sacque that I recognized as Miss Sophia's. "That's Maria Therese," said Celeste. "She's not Jane's mother, though. Her mother isn't here. Nobody knows where she is. The other man is Maria's husband, Charles, and the man in the long cape, walking around with his teacup and reciting Shakespeare under his breath, is John Philip Kemble. That's Jane's father."

Everyone practically genuflected before them. Jane walked among them and spoke to them with a familiarity that we all admired. But I was not envious. I was glad of the confusion, for it changed the school routine. And I was filled with the new excitement, which lay like a basket of warm, fresh-baked bread before me, of having found my own father.

The butlers and maids, who were usually watching us, scarcely knew that we existed. Miss Sophia was absent altogether, and not likely to soon return. Miss Harriet was busy with her guests. All this made for possibilities, and every girl was aware of it.

Around me, I heard whispering, plans about going out. But how would we get out? It was Miss Harriet who made it possible for all of us. She called me aside. "It would be a good idea for you girls to make another charitable visit today, since there will be no school-work, wouldn't it?"

I agreed.

She smiled. And it was like a light in a mine shaft, although I'd never been in a mine shaft. "Go to him. Make use of your time," she said.

"Who?"

"The man you met yesterday. Miss Sophia will be gone for a few days, and I'll have my hands full for a while keeping these people supplied with clean linen, black pudding, scones, and fresh fish. Tell the other girls this is their schoolwork for now. Ask Callie for the medicines and supplies to take with you."

The door knocker constantly banged. People came and went, offering donations on the spot for the rehabilitation of the theater, suggesting fairs to raise money, and not above taking a plate of food as they presented their plans.

I told the other girls. And they were just as glad for a chance to be out of the school as I was. Jane, of course, was excused from the exercise, but she volunteered to go about the square and summon the chaperones. "And in your spare time, study," Miss Harriet said as she walked away. "We have examinations before Christmas. And they are very important."

Upstairs, Lizzy came to me.

"I need something from you," she said.

"Yes?"

"In view of what I know," she went on, "and what chaos it would cause you if anyone here, much less the rest of London, knew, I thought you would listen."

"I'm listening, Lizzy."

"Well, in examinations we'll be questioned individually."

"Yes."

"We'll be called in according to our last names."

"They don't go by last names in this school, because they're not really sure of anybody's last name. We're all such liars," I said.

"They know more than you think they do. They know who's paying the bills, and that's the last name they go by. And Mary Christian comes before Lizzy Lamb."

"The Curwens pay my bills."

"Which means the same thing. You still come before me."

"What is it you want, Lizzy?"

"You know."

I sighed. I did know. Still, I would make her say it. I'd not say it for her.

"I want you to tell me the questions they ask," she said.

"But that isn't honorable," I said innocently.

Lizzy laughed. "How many other girls do you think are making such arrangements? You'll do it, Mary Christian, or the whole school will know your father is alive and in Guy's Hospital. And soon afterward, the whole of London will know. Well?"

Honor, honor. That's all my family had worried about when I left home. That I should do nothing to sully the family honor. And now Lizzy was asking me to do just that.

But what if I didn't comply with her wishes? Wouldn't the family honor be sullied then, if my father was captured and the whole thing brought to light again?

Grandmother wouldn't be able to live through such an ordeal. Oh, what to do?

But I knew. And Lizzy knew what I would do. I must dishonor a six-hundred-year-old name in order to save it.

"All right," I said, "I'll do it."

I went to dress for the trip to Guy's Hospital.

We brought some books, writing paper and ink, and another change of clothing to the hospital this time. It seemed impossible to me that I was bringing clothing to my father, the officer in His Majesty's Navy, the son of Grandmother, the descendant of justices, governors, lords, and rulers.

It seemed impossible when I saw his face that he was all this. But then, in the next moment, it seemed possible again. There was something about him—his carriage; his long, slender hands; the way he held his head; his eyes—that bespoke generations of breeding.

179

Willy was my savior that day.

"I see you are taking care of these girls," my father said to Willy. And I read between the lines: *I see you are taking care of my daughter.*

"Yes, sir," Willy said.

But Willy knew more. This young man, for I regarded him as no less by now, not only knew most people on London's streets, but he read them, knowing of their goodness or badness. It was the way he survived.

And he knew that Dr. Katterfelt was my father. He had known it before I did.

I did not ask him how. I only took him aside and asked him to take Lizzy out, to leave me alone with the man. So he suggested to Lizzy that she visit another man in the hospital, and get her own credit instead of sharing mine.

Lizzy agreed. What did she care? She already had my promise of dishonor.

⤳ SIXTEEN

It was less than a month before Christmas. Already girls were making plans to go home, that is, those who had homes—those who didn't would stay. It was said that the Misses Harriet and Sophia made as nice a holiday as could be for them. I wanted to stay. And then, in the next moment, I wanted to go home. I missed Uncle Charles and Gwen and my town of Douglas, which seemed so far away now, almost as if it had never existed.

Then two letters came. One was from the Curwens, inviting me to Ewanrigg, their winter home. And one was from Grandmother, telling me to accept the invitation, that she was feeling under the weather and could not possibly put on a show of gaiety for the holidays.

I would be just as glad to stay put. My father was here in London. I didn't want to go home. I'd write to the Curwens and decline politely. I'd say I was doing a charitable project and had to stay. They would like that.

But if Grandmother did not want me home, did that mean something was wrong? I wrote both to her and to Uncle Charles and told them I was busy with a charitable project and wanted to stay. They wrote back. Both were now in fine fettle, so my conscience was clear. Uncle Charles said, "Attend to your project." He'd have Gwen accompany him on his rounds to bring gifts of food or clothing to the poor, and they'd send my gifts to the school.

Three people besides me knew of my father's existence, and that was three too many. Willy knew, Lizzy knew, and Miss Harriet knew something. I could trust Willy and Miss Harriet. As for Lizzy, she'd have me confined to Newgate in a minute for looking at her the wrong way. I must be careful.

Weeks had passed since the fire at Covent Garden Theatre, and we had returned to our lessons. Even so, I went twice more to see my father.

Part of the project was to take the person we had selected under our wing. Willy did his part. He helped repair Dr. Katterfelt's coach, which sat outside the hospital, next to a shed. It had a broken wheel and axle, and seemed forlorn and abandoned.

Besides bringing food and medicines and clothing, we and our chaperones were to find our charges a place to live. And work.

My project was easy on that count. Dr. Katterfelt already had a profession and a place to live, though I did not know where.

Jane, who was back with us, and Fanny had teamed up to help a mother of two who was in prison for stealing loaves of bread for her little ones.

Sibella and Alice were working with a woman at Newgate imprisoned for another minor crime. If it had not been for the project, she would have been shipped to Australia with a boatload of women prisoners. Celeste and her chaperone were finding homes for two children at Christ's Hospital, which was also an orphanage. So all the girls were saving somebody, except for Lizzy and me. She didn't care, and all I wanted was to get Dr. Katterfelt to admit that he was my father.

On the second visit, I told Lizzy she ought to take on the other person she was visiting, an old lady who was near death. "We have to write papers, remember."

"I'll use what I have," she said.

"And what have you, then?" I felt the hand of terror gripping my innards.

"Well, I could write something romantic, and say who I think he is."

"You wouldn't!"

"Not if you give me two hours today to wander about at will. I never have been on London's streets alone, you know."

"I'll go wit' 'er," Willy said.

"I don't want you!" she snapped.

"Oh, yeah? You want to git bitten by a mad dog? Kidnapped and made a slave? It's yer choice."

She relented.

"She's blackmailin' ye, lass," Willy whispered before they left.

"I know she is. She's been doing it all along," I whispered back as I prepared to go inside. "It's all right, Willy. I can handle her."

"I have money," Lizzy boasted. "We can get some hot buns and cider from a vendor."

"Or ye kin give it to a footpad when he snatches it from ye," Willy said.

They went off. I went inside.

I had brought paper, ink, and a quill pen. I would make notes for my paper.

"How are you today, Dr. Katterfelt?"

"I'm tolerable, miss."

"You should call me Mary." After all, I thought, you named me such. "I've brought you some ham and buns. And more medicines. How is your leg?"

"My leg is fine. The arm is bothering me."

"What happened to your arm?"

"I banged it when I fell. Didn't feel anything for a week after, but now it's giving me the Devil's own pain."

"Do you need a bandage? Let me see."

He drew away. He had been unbuttoning his sleeve to see the arm himself, and it was then that I saw the tattoo on his forearm. It was of a woman.

A native woman.

He saw that I saw it, and hurriedly pulled down his sleeve.

A look passed between us like the sun on a blazing hot day. Then the room darkened, as if the sun had gone behind a cloud to hide.

I reached inside my basket. "I have some laudanum if you need it."

He took the powders and thanked me. "I'm not your father, Mary. I was on a ship in the merchant service. We stopped at some islands is all."

"Yes, sir," I said.

"Don't call me sir!" he snapped.

I stared at him. Tears came to my eyes.

"I'm sorry, child. I just can't say I'm your father."

"Can't? Or won't?" I asked.

"Can't, because I'm not."

"You're lying."

"I beg your pardon?" And he drew himself up as a father would, and scowled.

"Now you look just like Uncle Charles when I've done something wrong," I told him.

He turned away. "What are the paper and pen for?" he said, giving the conversation a new turn.

"I have to write a paper on my project. On you."

"Well, write away, then."

"I have to ask questions."

"Ask away."

That surprised me. I set the paper on my lap, the ink bottle where it wouldn't spill, and started to ask questions. "Where did you come from?"

"I was born in the north of London."

Everything he told me was a lie, and likely what

he'd told them here at the hospital, for it was well rehearsed.

Then he asked me about my life, and I told him about Douglas, my school there, Uncle Charles's living in his surgery, everything. I told him how Uncle Edward had come to the school and washed my mouth out with soap. He scowled at that. I told him of Grandmother and Gwen, of Langston and the Curwens. How my brother, Thursday October, had written to me.

He lowered his head when I spoke of the Curwens. He told me to write back to my brother. I hesitated.

"He hasn't had your advantages," he said.

I promised him I would.

Then it was time to go, and I left with a heavy heart.

"I hope you do well on your paper," he said.

He'd be back on the streets soon. I knew that. What would happen then? Would he still come to our school as Dr. Katterfelt? Or would I never see him again?

I waited outside the front gate until Willy and Lizzy came. She had purchases in hand, books and candy. Willy hailed a carriage, and we went home.

Examinations!

They determined if a girl could stay in the school. For all the progressive thoughts of our teachers, they still felt they had to show we were learning.

It would be only me and Celeste for the holidays. All the girls were leaving, even Lizzy. She'd been invited home by her father. We had so much in common, she and I, that it was a shame we couldn't be friends. We both yearned for our fathers. But at least hers admitted who he was. And yet she complained.

I stayed up late to study, although we'd been told not to. The Kembles were gone, and we were back in our own rooms again. Christmas was only two weeks away. Already the girls who were leaving had packed and would depart right after examinations.

I was getting excited about Christmas. After all, its promise was rich. Miss Sophia and Miss Harriet had promised us the theater in Drury Lane, the opera at the Haymarket, visits to tearooms, a concert at St. Paul's, and even puppet shows.

Papers from our projects were turned in. All we had to do now was write a list of our blessings—considering that we knew what they were now, after visiting such dolorous places.

I had begged for, and received, permission to visit Dr. Katterfelt one more time. My teachers humored me in my request because of who he was. They knew him and wanted him back on the street with his scientific lessons.

But the oral examinations! Oh, what would the questions be? We played guessing games.

"How does the theater identify with British beliefs and values?" Celeste guessed.

"Is it immune to foreign influence?" said Sibella.

"It won't be all about theater," said Fanny. "What did James Watt write to Erasmus Darwin?"

"Oh, I know, I know," Jane said. "How did the French contribute, both in chemistry and in politics?"

I put my own question in. "Where does the word *suitable* begin and end when it comes to women's education?"

And yet the Misses Hartsdale might not touch on any of these things at all. I could not be sure what they would ask. I was sure of only one thing. I would come out of my own examination knowing that I had to tell the questions to Lizzy. Or suffer the consequences.

After the examinations, we were supposed to retire to our rooms and take a nap. Tea would be brought to us on a tray. We would have special cake. There was to be no running or talking to one another upstairs.

I quickly retired to my room after my examination, convinced I had failed, but more concerned with getting my questions down on paper for Lizzy. I would use the water closet and leave the folded-up paper there, behind the necessary.

That was the plan.

Then I was to leave for my final visit to Dr. Katterfelt. Willy was to take me.

I scribbled furiously, hating myself all the while. Then I made a trip to the water closet, flushed the necessary for effect, and hid the questions. There would be time enough for Lizzy to look things up if she didn't know them. She had all the books in her room.

I knew that if found out, I would be put out of school. It would mean dishonor for my family, the first act of dishonor since my father had done his mutiny.

Grandmother would cry. Uncle Charles would look away, then scold and punish me. Uncle Edward would say, "Well, what do you expect? I told you she is the perfect example of original sin, didn't I?"

That worried me the most. That Uncle Edward would be right.

Oh, I hated Lizzy!

But what if it was spread about that my father was here in England, wanted by the King? His fame would spread faster through the town than if heralded by trumpeters.

I was doing this for my family, wasn't I?

"Following in his footsteps," I could hear Uncle Edward saying. "There is no excuse for dishonor."

I put on my cloak and bonnet and went quietly downstairs to the kitchen, where my basket of remedies and food awaited me. Then I went out back to find Willy.

I was silent all the way there. This time we took the school carriage, with the name of the school scrolled in fancy script on the side door. Miss Harriet and Miss Sophia always said that the school name and the emblem below it would keep the occupants safe on the streets. Holton, the stablemaster, drove. As the carriage rocked through London's streets, the now familiar sights no longer moved me, not even a gang of ruffian boys fighting in the middle of Liverpool Street.

Willy got down from the carriage, went among them, and broke up the fight before the magistrates arrived. It turned out that they knew him.

"Hey, Willy," we heard as Willy climbed back inside the carriage, "where ye been?"

"Fancy carriage there, hey wot?"

"Who's the lass?"

"Willy's in school. Either that or 'e's got hisself a bloody fortune."

"Look at them clothes!"

"Hey, Willy, Old Nettlemouth is lookin' fer ye. 'E's got a reward out. Says 'e's goin' to slit yer throat."

"Who is Old Nettlemouth?" I asked when he was back in.

"Me old boss. The rat master."

"Hey, Willy, whatcha doin' at that fancy school?" They threw mud and stones and refuse from the street at us as we drove away.

"Now these boys know where I am," Willy muttered. "That ain't good."

"But they're your friends," I reminded him.

He did not answer, which was answer enough. We rode on, both silent and glum, both with our own problems. I didn't suppose I had ever felt as low in spirit as I did that morning, knowing what I had done in school. If I had been a boy, I would have run away. Ten-year-old boys can sign on as a ship captain's servant, Uncle Charles had once told me. Oh, how I wished I could confide in somebody! Inside me, in the place where our spirit dwells, I thought I was dying. And I couldn't bother Willy with it. To him, it would be trivial; somebody wanted to kill him.

By the time we got to the hospital, I could scarcely speak. "I'd like to be alone with Dr. Katterfelt," I told Willy.

Willy understood. He walked me inside dutifully and then disappeared. "An hour," he told me. "You have an hour. Sorry, lass, I gotta be back. I gotta git the horses to the blacksmith this afternoon." He was worried.

I nodded and went in to see Dr. Katterfelt.

He was eating hospital food, sitting at a small table, the sleeves of his white ruffled shirt turned up at the cuffs. As soon as he saw me, he stood and rolled down his sleeves, buttoned them, and gave a little bow.

"Hello," I said.

And then I burst into tears and ran to him, into his arms.

His arms enfolded me. He smelled of freshly laundered clothing and tobacco. "What is it, child?"

"I've done something terrible," I wailed.

"So have we all, at one time or another. Tell me, if you wish."

"I've dishonored my family!"

"You?" And he gave a short, bitter laugh. "You bring nothing but honor to your family, from what I can see. How could you not? What have you done, stolen a pretty from a street vendor?"

His voice had a tone of sadness that made me look up. He smiled dourly. "Tell me."

"I've helped a girl cheat at school."

"How?"

I told him.

He released me and sat on the edge of his bed. "Lord love a duck," he said. "You did this because you think I'm your father? And you're afraid she'll tell?"

"I did it to defend you. Even if you're not and she tells, you're in trouble with the authorities."

"You're right there, child. Oh, 'An orphan's curse

would drag to hell a spirit from on high,'" he said.

I stepped forward. "That's from *The Rime of the Ancient Mariner*," I said.

"Yes, it is."

I let the tears roll down my face. I stood sobbing quietly. He did not know what to do. "There is no excuse for dishonor," he said.

I nodded mutely. "I know."

"I know better than you, lass. You'll carry it with you all your life. An albatross around your neck."

"Yeess," I blubbered. And I thought: Like in *The Rime of the Ancient Mariner*. He knows.

Was he scolding like a true father, then? No, he was simply telling me, not judging me. Because he knew of dishonor.

He knew.

He wore the albatross around his neck. The same albatross the Mariner wore.

"And when people tell you how fine you are," he went on, "you'll flinch inside."

I nodded.

"And you'll wish to give any shilling you have, to rid yourself of the dishonor."

I said nothing, just wiped my face with my hand and gulped.

So there we were, in that miserable little room of his, locked in our mutual agony, he with his and I with mine, and somehow they were the same. And he did not scold, no. He commiserated with me.

Then he put his arms out, and I went to him. "Nothing you can do," he said, "but make the best of the hell you are in. There are times it won't be so bad. And times it will consume you. And you'll spend the rest of your life trying to make up for it."

"Yes, sir," I said.

We spoke for a while. He said all the right things except for admitting that he was my father. It was understood between us somehow, though. And then we said good-bye. He said he was getting back to the streets soon. He had to earn money. He wanted to go to America.

↶ EIGHTEEN

Willy and I left, and I felt like a wounded soldier. I could not even stand up straight. I might never see him again! America! He might go to America! Why would anybody go there?

Oh, I knew. Because all kinds of people who were running from something went there. Because you didn't have to worry about class distinctions. We'd learned that in school. But America! Why didn't he say the moon?

I got home to find out that everyone who was leaving for Christmas had left. I had forgotten about Christmas. How could we have it? I'd just as soon forgo the pleasures.

"Ye'll look fer 'im on the street. On the square, 'e'll be about," Willy told me. How I envied Willy. He had no attachments. He could turn his feelings on and off about people. I must have voiced my despair to him, because he said, "Don't worry. 'E'll be about."

It was the most Willy could give.

It was just Celeste and me in the house now, and she was such a quiet, mousy little thing that I knew the onus would be on me to keep her cheery. I looked across the table at her that night in the girls' dining room. "Who came for Lizzy?" I asked.

"I don't know. A hackney carriage. How is Dr. Katterfelt?"

"He's middling well. I suppose he'll be back on the streets soon."

"We should invite him for the holiday."

"Why didn't I think of that?" And then we both looked at each other in silence, imagining the man in his black clothes in the house with all those cats. And we smiled at each other.

I didn't tell her he would soon be going to America. Nobody should know that Fletcher Christian, mutineer and outlaw, had fled to America, if the connection between the two was made. To be sure, the King had no more power in America, but the United States and

Britain were having commerce with each other again. Didn't that mean my father could be sent back, if found?

I didn't know, and I didn't want to think about it. "Tell me about your family," I asked Celeste.

She gave a small smile. "You never ask."

"I'm asking now."

"My mother and father were French liberals. And when Mama came to London with me after Louis the Sixteenth was executed, she acted ashamed and was downcast for a long time. She taught me always to be quiet and good, and not to make a spectacle of myself or draw attention in any way. She thinks people are still watching us."

I nodded. "I wondered why you were so quiet. I thought you were shy."

"No. People here didn't like French liberals. They were afraid the same kind of revolution would take hold in England. Did you know that Louis the Sixteenth's last words were drowned out by drums, on purpose? And that the Dauphin begged mercy for his father in front of the Convention, and he was only eight?"

I shivered. "No." And I thought I had troubles with my father.

"My father was executed the day before. Do you think it hurts to have your head cut off?"

"I never thought about it."

"I asked Alice. She said if the executioner is good, it doesn't. She said that before he does the act, he begs forgiveness from the person about to be executed. Is that true?"

"I've heard that, yes."

"My father would have forgiven him."

We were allowed to stay up as late as we wanted that night, but we were both so exhausted, we retired at our usual time.

The next day we made a Christmas cake for Dr. Katterfelt. We soaked it in rum and wrapped it in cheesecloth. Miss Harriet, who could knit faster than anybody I knew, made him a new black scarf.

Right before Christmas, he came around in his black carriage again.

We had just come home from the Christmas concert at St. Paul's and were filled with the peace and hope that music gives to the soul. Miss Harriet had taken us. Miss Sophia was writing.

Callie had lit a blazing fire in the hearth in the front

parlor, and we'd just finished our tea when the sound of his horses' hooves clattered in the square.

"Ohhh, he's here!" cried Celeste, who had entered into the mood of waiting for him. "I'll go and get the cake."

I ran to the door, but Miss Harriet stopped me and made us put on cloaks. The wind outside was cold. The sky was heavy with the threat of snow. We wrapped ourselves well and took the gifts out to him.

"Oh, lovely, lovely!" he exclaimed. "I love Christmas, don't you?" He reached inside his pocket and then handed me a package. "To my little friend," he said.

I clutched it to my breast. Would it be a present from him as my project? Or from him as my father? Then, seeing Celeste, he threw up his hands and declared he could not forget her. And he produced a black kitten from inside his coat and handed it over. It mewed.

Celeste was enchanted. She cuddled the kitten close.

Over her head, he smiled at me. Then he presented Miss Harriet with a tin of tea. "I wish I had more for you ladies, but this tea is special," he said. "Good bohea."

I gasped. The tin was exactly like the ones Uncle Charles had that he sometimes gave to me and

Grandmother. But when Dr. Katterfelt again smiled at me, I saw he did not realize I knew about the tea.

I stood there, overcome with all kinds of feelings I could not sort out. Father, why won't you tell me who you are? I wanted to scream it out to the gray heavens.

But then Miss Harriet handed him a stone jar. "Cream for your cats for Christmas," she said.

Oh, why hadn't I thought of that?

"They will enjoy it." He took Miss Harriet's hand. Then he hugged Celeste and leaned toward me. I held my breath as he hugged me, but it was not a father's hug. It was a gentlemanly, formal hug.

And then he got back into the carriage, spoke to his horses, and was gone.

We went back into the house. I opened my gift. It was a packet of ribbons, blue and green, yellow and pink. I would wear one every day, I decided. Celeste put her kitten down on the rug, and he reached for the ribbons. Then we got busy making a bed for him. And a box to serve as his necessary, with ripped-up paper in it. "I'll get some sawdust from the stable later," I said.

We read for a while, the kitten playing between us on the couch in front of the fire. Then Celeste started to doze off, and the kitten fell asleep on her lap. I put on my cloak to go outside and get the sawdust.

Just as I was making my way to the stable, I heard a shout. It was Willy's voice, near the gate at the side of the back garden.

Beyond the rim of lamplight in the street, I could see two figures struggling with each other. Someone was attacking Willy!

"Willy!" I called. "Willy!"

Scully was barking and snapping and racing around them. I must do something! No one else was about.

"Go inside!" Willy shouted. "Take Scully!"

A large, burly man was wrestling Willy to the ground. A shot of fear went through me. Old Nettlemouth! The boys had told him where Willy lived, likely for a reward.

As they rolled toward me, I saw, under the lamplight, a gleaming knife in the larger man's hand. I tried to grab Scully, but he wouldn't be grabbed. So I did my best to pull the man off Willy. I got a good purchase on his greatcoat. It looked bulky, and things rattled when I grabbed it. It seemed full of things. Then I realized that the man had *inside* pockets. Willy had told me thieves did.

"Fistface!" I heard the man yell. "Fistface! Get this wench offa me."

I'd been aware of a horse and carriage in the darkness of the street, but hadn't paid mind to it. Out of the carriage came another man now, who grabbed me from behind, his arms around my waist. In a second I was off the ground, kicking and thrashing. Scully was nipping at Fistface's feet, to no avail.

Then Fistface carried me out of the lamplight and into the street. I yelled, but his large hand was clamped over my mouth.

In back of the houses facing St. James's Square were stables and tradesmen's shops, all silent in the night. If I could have screamed louder, someone would have come, I was sure of it. Helpless, I was carried to the carriage.

"I'll teach ye to go at me master, you little fancy," my captor whispered in my ear. "You're a sweet thing, ain't ye? Just the kind we need to draw the men in." And he lifted my cloak and put it over my head.

He was going to kidnap me!

I kicked wildly. This could not happen so close to my school. This could not happen! I tried again to scream, but only succeeded in getting the wool of my cloak in my mouth. I was being lifted into the carriage. I was helpless.

I never got there.

"Let her go, or this pistol in your ribs will put a bullet in your heart."

I was suspended in midair, then dropped gracelessly to the ground, where I landed on my right shoulder and the right side of my head. And that is all I remember.

"She's coming around." Miss Harriet's voice.

"Mary, darling, open your eyes, please." Miss Sophia.

"Come on, Mary, child, please." My father's.

I was dead, that was it. My fall had killed me and I was in heaven. But what were the others doing here?

I couldn't open my eyes, simply because my head hurt so. But my father's voice was there again, in front of me, pulling me out of my hazy, comfortable place.

"Mary." The tone so deep and strong and full of love that I forced my eyes open. All was blue at first. Then I saw Miss Harriet's face, grinning at me. "Some people will do anything to get attention," she said.

"Are you all right, dear?" Miss Sophia asked. "The doctor was here. He bandaged your head. Your face will be swollen for a few days, but you'll be all right."

"My shoulder hurts."

"He said it wasn't broken. Only bruised."

My arm was in a sling.

"Mary, can you see?" This from my father.

"Yes."

"Here. The doctor left you powders." He gave me one with some water. "Now we both have hurt arms," he said softly.

"Willy!" It came to me then. "Is Willy all right?"

"I'm right 'ere," came his reply. He stepped forward. He, too, had a bandaged head. And hand. "Did he cut you with that terrible knife?" I asked.

He shrugged. "I've 'ad worse."

Oh, Dr. Katterfelt—my father?—was so dear! I wanted to hug him, but I had trouble just sitting up. They propped pillows behind me. What had happened, it turned out, was that after Dr. Katterfelt left us, he had driven his carriage around to the back of the square, had some commerce with friends he knew there, and then witnessed the fight Willy was having and saw my being carried off.

Celeste had fallen asleep and heard none of it. Miss Harriet and Miss Sophia were in their office in front of the house, writing.

If it had not been for Dr. Katterfelt, Scully, at my feet now, would be fighting rats again. I'd have been carried off to some kind of slavery for Old Nettlemouth, and Willy would be dead.

I could not contemplate it. It was all too strange. Dr. Katterfelt stayed awhile. He was fed and fussed over. I lay on the couch, half dozing from the powder and struggling to keep my eyes open and to watch my father. Willy sat on the floor, eating with his one good hand, with Scully next to him.

When Dr. Katterfelt came to say good-bye, I looked into his face. "Will I see you again?"

"Yes, child. Here, I forgot to give you this before."

"What is it?"

"Guard it well," he whispered. Then he was gone.

NINETEEN

I did not see him again.

I shall see him someday. Because of what was in the package he gave me.

In it was money for a voyage on a ship to America. Also instructions.

I was to finish my schooling first. It would give him time to get himself settled and in a position to care for me. He might settle in Washington City. After all, he had a cousin there, a Thomas Law, who had wed a step-granddaughter of the late George Washington. I was to stay at my school and study well.

I was to give the utmost respect to Grandmother

and Uncle Charles. And even to Uncle Edward. They had been informed of his plans.

Uncle Charles would decide when I was ready to travel to America. But I would go only if I wanted, truly, to go. The gravity of the parting with my loved ones would be explained to me.

In the meantime I was to work and play, grow and learn.

If I went, I could bring a servant, if I wished. And it might be well if I brought along Willy also, to guard us.

I must never, under pain of estrangement from him, tell anyone that Dr. Katterfelt had gone to America.

I must give my best wishes to the Curwens, and honor them always.

And oh, yes. The last time I had been there, to Belle Isle? He had been the butler. He had begged the Curwens to allow him to play the role, just to see me.

I wrote to Gwen, asking her if she would come to America with me. "Your troll was right," I wrote. "I am going to take you on a long voyage someday. Farther than London."

She wrote back, saying yes and asking, "Are there trolls in America?"

I said yes, I supposed trolls had made their way there.

I never made friends with Lizzy. But I got my letter from Thursday October back. I stole it, as she stole it from me. So she no longer has sway over me. And I wrote to Thursday October. I gave the letter to Willy, to give to a ship's captain who was leaving for the Pacific Ocean. If it got to Pitcairn at all, it must travel ship to ship.

Dick Turpin still likes me. But he chases Pluto, Celeste's kitten, all over the house.

Miss Harriet says she will never forgive herself because her second sight failed her that night when I was nearly kidnapped. But then she says that she supposes if she had rescued me, Dr. Katterfelt never would have.

I still dream of ships. All kinds of ships. I wonder if I'll dream of them when I'm on one, going to America.

Dr. Katterfelt never, anywhere in the letter he left me, allowed that he was my father.

As I wrote in the foreword ("Read This First"), no one has been able to find Fletcher Christian's grave on Pitcairn Island, although his descendants there vow he was killed and buried there.

But, with no grave, legend has grown, and as Christian has evolved as a hero in English and American folklore, his legend has been nurtured and lives. It has been said since 1796 that he returned to England. There have been numerous books and movies about him, although they are mostly concerned with the mutiny. Yet only two books that I know of, *Mister Christian* by William Kingsolving and *Isabella* by

Fiona Mountain, have him returning to England. And neither deals with his daughter, Mary.

Mary was my own contribution to the legend. However, everything I wrote about the Isle of Man was as I interpreted it to have been from scholarly books and research on the Internet. Likewise everything I wrote about the Christian family and its noble past.

While Fletcher Christian's mother did not run a lodging house in her later years, she certainly did live on Man, in circumstances reduced from those she had known in her earlier life. Fletcher's brother Charles was exactly as I depicted him: unmarried, a physician who'd been to sea as a ship's surgeon, and who indeed took part in a mutiny. Uncle Edward also was as I described him: a barrister living in London who was partially responsible for bankrupting his mother and who, together with his brother John, spent his father's money even before Fletcher was grown to manhood.

Everything about the Christian family as I have written it is true.

Indeed, the family itself—its background, its accomplishments, and its holdings, and relationships—is a real find for a novelist.

The Curwens also are true to life, as is Belle Isle. It is said that Fletcher had a romance with his cousin Isabella, but that since he had no position and no riches, he had to go to sea and she married John Curwen, the man who had helped Fletcher's mother financially over the years.

Edward Christian did write a book defending the Christian name after the court-martial of the men found on Tahiti and brought back for trial. (At this time Fletcher was not found because he was on Pitcairn Island.)

Only Mary's return to England and her schooling and life are invented for the sake of story. No one really knows what happened to Fletcher Christian. He was seen back in Plymouth, on the wharves, by Peter Heywood in 1808, but when Peter called out to him, he turned, then ran.

He did have that peculiar gait that all the Christian men had. He did cross his *t*'s the same way as his brother Charles.

All the folklore I described in this book, as practiced and believed on the Isle of Man, is accurate. There is a wealth of folklore on this enchanted isle, most of which I did not even tap into. The incident about Gwen being lost, then found in the rock formation above Pigeon Stream, is based on that folklore.

I have tried to depict London of the early nineteenth century as accurately as possible. The Covent Garden Theatre did burn at this time; there were "rat boys" like Willy in the streets, as well as chimney sweeps and hundreds of homeless children. There were peddlers. Dr. Katterfelt is based on a Dr. Katterfelto, whom I found during my research, in *Daily Life in 18th-Century England* by Kirstin Olsen.

All the girls in the school, as well as life in the school and the Misses Harriet and Sophia, are my own invention. Schoolgirls at this time had much less freedom. Samuel Taylor Coleridge's *Rime of the Ancient Mariner* was written, some people say, about Fletcher Christian. This only adds to the romance of the legend surrounding the mutineer. I could not resist including him in my book, so I have Coleridge coming to visit Mary's school. Everything he tells the girls about himself on this visit is true.

It was said that Mary Christian was a beautiful young woman. The words describing her in the book are taken from accounts of the time.

Nowhere is it said that Fletcher Christian fled to

America. That is my own invention too. But there are many with the Christian name in America. If he indeed came back to England, he couldn't have stayed and been recognized. So he fled somewhere. Why not, I thought, America?

~~ *Bibliography*

Christian, Glynn. *Fragile Paradise: The Discovery of Fletcher Christian, Bounty Mutineer.* London: Hamish Hamilton Ltd., 1982.

Coleridge, Samuel Taylor. *The Rime of the Ancient Mariner.* New York: Dover Publications, 1970 (among many other editions).

Ellis, Amanda M. *Rebels and Conservatives: Dorothy and William Wordsworth and Their Circle.* Bloomington, Indiana: Indiana University Press, 1967.

George, M. Dorothy. *London Life in the Eighteenth Century.* Chicago: Academy Chicago Publishers, 1984.

Hough, Richard. *Captain Bligh and Mister Christian: The Men and the Mutiny.* Annapolis, Maryland: Naval Institute Press, 1972.

Kingsolving, William. *Mister Christian*. New York: Simon & Schuster, 1996.

Lefebure, Molly. *Samuel Taylor Coleridge: A Bondage of Opium*. Briarcliff Manor, New York: Stein and Day, 1974.

McCalman, Iain, ed. *An Oxford Companion to the Romantic Age: British Culture, 1776–1832*. Oxford and New York: Oxford University Press, 1999.

Mountain, Fiona. *Isabella*. Long Preston, England: Magna Large Print Books, 2001.

Olsen, Kirstin. *Daily Life in 18th-Century England*. Westport, Connecticut: Greenwood Press, 1999.

SINCE 1911

Donated by
Floyd Dickman